Green, Tim,
     1963-

Football genius.

DATE			

FOOTBALL
GENIUS

FOO
GE

HarperCollins*Publishers*

Library of Congress Cataloging-in-Publication Data

Green, Tim, date

Football genius / Tim Green. — 1st ed.

p. cm.

Summary: Troy, a sixth grader with an unusual gift for predicting football plays before they occur, attempts to use his ability to help his favorite team, the Atlanta Falcons, but he must first prove himself to the coach and players.

ISBN 978-0-06-112270-5 (trade bdg.)

ISBN 978-0-06-112272-9 (lib. bdg.)

[1. Football—Fiction. 2. Atlanta (Ga.)—Fiction.] I. Title.

PZ7.G826357Foo 2007   2006029470

[Fic]—dc22   CIP

                                                                              AC

Typography by Joel Tippie

5 6 7 8 9 10

❖

First Edition

*For my five kids: Thane, Tessa, and Ty,
who inspired me with their love for reading, and to
the real Troy and Tate, who made writing this book a
pure joy, breathing life into the story with
their ideas and assistance*

"It is time for us all to stand and cheer for the doer, the achiever—the one who recognizes the challenges and does something about it."
—*Vince Lombardi*

CHAPTER ONE

TROY KNEW IT WAS wrong. It was wrong to sneak out of the house after midnight. It was wrong to take something that wasn't yours. And, even though he wasn't that kind of kid, that night, he was doing both.

Usually, on a night like that night, the crickets' end-of-summer song and the moths bumping against the window screen would put him to sleep. Usually, he didn't hear his mom turn off the TV in the living room. And usually, if he was up *that* late, the water groaning through the pipes while his mom ran her bath would finish him off. But that night, worry kept him awake. Because he really wasn't the kind of kid to sneak out, and especially to take something that wasn't his.

1

But if he did have to quietly slide open the screen, straddle the window, and drop to the ground with a thud, this was a good night to do it. Stars swirled around the big yellow moon, casting shadows perfect for hiding. Shorts and a T-shirt were all he needed to stay warm.

He didn't plan on having to run, but he laced his sneakers tight in case he did. His feet fell without a sound over the path through the pine trees. He could smell the trees' sticky sap, still warm from the hot September day. An owl hooted somewhere close. A rabbit screamed, then went quiet. The crickets stopped, and only the buzz of mosquitoes filled the air.

Troy looked back at his house. It was nestled into the pines, with no side or backyard. In front, there was nothing more than a gritty patch of red clay. A tire hung from a limb at the edge of the patch. A target for footballs. The house was more like a cabin, a single-story box with a roof covered by fallen pine needles.

Still, the weak orange glow from the night-light in the bathroom window was like a friend, calling him back. Away from the owl and the mosquitoes.

But Troy had other friends, and he dodged through the pine trees into the darkness, finding his way to the railroad tracks almost without looking. He stood on the steel rail, balancing his sneakers and looking down the long line toward the Pine Grove apartment complex, where his friends lived. He tried to whistle, but it came out wrong. He tried again, and again, before giving up.

"Tate?" he called, first soft, then louder. "Tate."

A whistle came back at him from the woods, high and clear, the way you'd call a dog. In the light of the moon, he watched two figures climb up the stony railway bed and start walking his way on the tracks. One of the figures was as thin as the rail she balanced on. Tate McGreer, a pretty girl with dark eyes, olive skin, and silky brown hair tied into a ponytail.

The other was big and burly. A twelve-year-old in the body of a high school kid. Nathan had a buzz cut like his dad and he liked to laugh, big belly laughs. He wasn't laughing now. His eyes were wide and shifting nervously, and he was puffing. Tate was the only one who stayed calm when they heard the low, sad sound of the coming train.

"The Midnight Express," Tate said, peering down the tracks. "It wakes me up almost every night. Atlanta to Chicago.

"Like clockwork."

They all scrambled back down the bank into the rocky ditch, and Tate chewed her gum and nudged them both and asked, "You got a penny?"

"A penny?" Troy said.

Nathan dug into his pocket and came up with a nickel.

"That'll work," she said, taking it from him and scrambling back up the side of the railroad bed.

The ground underneath them was rumbling now. The train's light glimmered and shook. Troy yelled at her to come back. She set the money down on the rail, glared at the train for a moment with her hands on her skinny hips, then hopped back down into the ditch with them.

When the train went by in a rush of hot air, it roared so loud, Troy had no idea what Tate was saying, even though he could see that she was shouting at the top of her lungs. As the last car clacked away down the tracks, he asked her what.

"You see how big that thing was? It's like a warning, right? Like 'go back,'" she said.

Her dark eyes sparkled in the moonlight. Nathan had his hands deep in the pockets of his cutoff shorts, and he nodded at her words. Troy thought about the rabbit he heard screaming in the dark.

"Don't go," he said, shrugging. "I'm not making you."

"We're not going *in*," Tate said, snapping her gum. "I said that. But we'll wait for you on the outside. That's what friends do. Moral support."

"You shouldn't stand on the tracks when the train's coming like that," Nathan said.

"Aw," she said, swatting air, "if they see a person, they slow right down. Jam their brakes on. Sparks everywhere."

She skipped up the bank again and lifted the flattened nickel up for them to see. It shone in the moonlight.

"Cool," Nathan said, taking it from her.

Troy went up and over the rail bed, leaving them behind.

"Don't you want to see it?" Tate asked, calling after him.

But his eyes were on the wall. Already through the trees he could see it. Ten feet high. Cool gray concrete. It surrounded the Cotton Wood Country Club. Tennis, golf, and five hundred of the most expensive homes in Atlanta. He had driven down Old River Road once, past the massive front gates and guardhouses on the other side. When he asked his mom if she'd ever been inside, she glanced at him and said it wasn't a place for people like them. She said he shouldn't spend his time wondering or worrying about it.

But sometimes, when the wind was right and he was outside throwing his football, he could hear things from inside the wall. Children laughing. The bark of a dog. Trash cans banging together. Sounds you could hear outside the wall too. So when Troy found the secret hole, he had to go in. No one knew about the hole except Tate and Nathan. Neither of them ever went in with him, and he never tried to take them, even though the reward for going in gave him goose bumps.

CHAPTER TWO

ONE OF THE RICH people who lived inside the wall was the Atlanta Falcons' star linebacker, Seth Halloway. Troy knew because he'd been there. In fact, every time he snuck through the wall, that was where he went. To Seth's house. To the big green backyard beyond Seth's pool.

It was a yard where players, real NFL players, would toss footballs to one another and goof around like Troy and his friends. Troy had watched them from the bushes. He'd seen them tossing footballs back and forth. Diving. Grabbing. Rolling on the ground and laughing. And he knew that Seth Halloway kept the balls in a mesh bag that hung from a nail underneath his deck. There were dozens of them. The first time Troy had seen Seth spill them out onto that big lawn, he felt his heart ache.

Now his heart was pounding. When they came to the hole—really just a big crack—the three of them stood and stared.

"Can't you just tell them your mom couldn't get the football?" Nathan asked.

Tate and Nathan loved football too. They all played together on the Duluth Tigers, a junior league team coached by fathers. Tate was the kicker. Nathan played on the line. Troy was the second-string quarterback. Nathan and Tate agreed that he should be first string, but Jamie Renfro's father was the coach, so Jamie got to be the Tigers' quarterback. In fact, it was because of Jamie that the three of them were out at night when they shouldn't have been.

It was hard for Troy, being second string when he was a better player than Jamie. Troy was faster, he had a better arm, and he practiced throwing almost every night. Besides, he knew the game way better than Jamie. He could read a defense in the blink of an eye and sometimes even seem to know what the other team was going to do. Tate and Nathan said it was a gift.

He couldn't explain how he knew. No one taught him. He just knew. But Troy didn't have a father of his own to be the coach, so he sat on the bench, calling the plays before they happened to his friends. And, while he really was a good kid, the situation with Jamie made him mad. Troy's mom sometimes called him a hothead. Sometimes she was right.

At Tuesday's practice, after standing by with his helmet off for ten plays in a row and watching Jamie throw a bad pass to the wrong receiver every time, Troy couldn't help himself. Jamie's father was yelling again. Yelling at the receivers. Yelling at the linemen. Everyone but Jamie. Jamie's father told them that yelling was what coaches did.

"Maybe he can coach you to throw a pass," Troy said as the kids on the first-string offense were getting into the huddle. He meant to say it low, but the hothead part of him made it too loud.

Jamie's freckled face went red behind his face mask. He walked out of the huddle and stood face-to-face with Troy, his dark, curly hair spilling out of the back of his helmet. Jamie was bigger than Troy. In fact, he was a whole year older even though he was still in seventh grade.

"At least I have a father," Jamie said.

Troy felt his eyes fill with tears, his real weakness. Even though he was tough and a good athlete, he sometimes couldn't stop the tears, no matter how hard he tried. His cheeks grew hot. He swallowed, stuck out his chin, and said, "My mom is worth ten fathers."

Jamie looked around with his mouth and eyes wide open, like he was in shock.

"That's funny," he said, wagging his head around. "I don't see her on the football field."

"She's on a football field that's a lot more important than this goat lot," Troy said.

"Right," Jamie said.

"She works for the Falcons," Troy said, swallowing and looking around.

"Since *when?*"

"Since she just started."

"I bet not."

"I bet so," Troy said, clenching his fists, ready in case Jamie said something bad about his mom.

"So good," Jamie said, grinning in a mean way. "She can get a Falcons football for the game Saturday. My dad's got one signed by Billy 'White Shoes' Johnson. He says the way you know a real Falcons ball is 'cause the team name is stamped right on it. It's cool. My dad's ball has it. Now your mom's a big shot working for the Falcons, man, she can get one for us to use, right?"

"She can get whatever I want," Troy said, and he looked past Jamie from Tate to Nathan. The pain in their faces made his stomach tight. They knew that he wasn't quite telling the truth about his mom.

There had been an ad in the newspaper for an assistant in the public relations department for the Falcons. Troy's mom had just finished getting her master's degree in public relations at night school that summer. One of her professors knew someone who got her an interview. She was one of ten. Troy got her to promise that if she got the job, she would somehow get him that ball.

The Tigers practiced every night during the week, and every night Jamie asked Troy where the ball was. And every night Troy said he'd have it for the game on Saturday.

When Troy got home from school on Friday, his mom was sitting at the kitchen table dunking a tea bag. She looked sad, but when she saw him, she smiled.

"What happened?" he asked, out of breath. "Did you get it?"

She shrugged and said, "Maybe. Now they're saying they might not know until tomorrow, or maybe Tuesday, after Labor Day."

Too late for the game. Too late to keep Jamie from laughing at him, telling everyone he was a liar, and flashing that nasty smile. That was too much for Troy to think about. Especially because of what he knew was on the other side of that wall. A mesh bag full of Falcons footballs. A bag so full, no one would miss just one.

That's why the three of them stood there in the moonlight, staring. That's why Troy didn't look at his friends as he ducked down and squeezed sideways through the dark hole.

Into a place he knew he shouldn't be.

CHAPTER THREE

TROY'S MOM HAD A saying she used all the time: "Some things are just meant to be."

He left his friends and dodged and ducked from tree to tree, from one clump of bushes to another, past the giant homes with their wrought-iron fences and their big swimming pools. It took ten minutes before he stood bent over with his hands on his knees, peering through the branches at the gray stone mansion where Seth Halloway lived.

It was meant to be.

A fountain trickled into Seth's pool and a raft floated along under the moonlight, bumping the stone side. The lawn was littered with footballs like strange Easter eggs in a magical land. Under the shadow of one giant oak tree was a JUGS machine, with its two tan rubber wheels that spun and fired footballs like bullets. It was an awkward machine that reminded Troy of a stork, with the motor and wheels perched at a funny angle on top of its three metal legs. NFL players used it to practice catching.

Troy looked up at the big house. Three scattered windows shone with yellow light, but nothing moved inside. He waited and watched, then realized if he kept waiting, he'd never do it. He thought about Jamie and that nasty smile. He took three deep breaths, counting them out loud. Then he ran out of the shadows and into the bright moonlight of the lawn.

He scooped up a ball and, clutching it tight, darted back into the bushes. Branches and brambles whipped his arms and face. Thorns bit at his bare legs. Still, he ran, plowing forward away from the house, heading for the wall.

Somehow, in the trees, he got turned around. When he burst through a hedgerow, he tripped and tumbled down a grassy bank, flat onto the blacktop of a street. He picked the gravel out of his mouth and got to his knees. He was wet, and it took him a minute to realize that the sprinklers were running. He heard the security truck before he saw its big white shape with the yellow light on top turn the corner and blind him in the glare of its headlights. Without thinking, he shot back up the bank, but his sneakers slipped on the grass. His feet shot out from under him and he tumbled back down.

The ball, wet and slick, popped out of his arms and rolled out into the street. The truck came to a stop, its headlights burning the pavement all around Troy. He shivered, partly from the chill, but mostly from fear. The door opened.

"Hey!" the security guard shouted. "You! Kid!"

Troy hesitated, but only for a second. He darted out into the street, scooped up the ball, and started to run. This time he stayed on the road.

Behind him, the truck door slammed and the engine revved up. Troy's legs were numb. He knew he was fast, but he didn't know he was that fast. He got to the end of the street and took a left, out of the car's head-light beams. He kept going, but there were no turnoffs, only driveways to the big homes, and soon the head-lights were on him again and the yellow light on top of the truck was flashing. Finally, he came to another intersection. This time he went right, and before the truck's lights could catch him, he jumped over a low hedge and flattened himself under some bushes.

His head thumped and his lungs burned. The truck eased past him and drove up the street. But then its taillights glowed red. It stopped and turned around, pulling up to where he hid, stopping on the street right in front of him. Its engine purred, and Troy heard the electric window hum down.

The car door opened and the security guard got out. When he crossed the beam of the headlights, Troy saw the blue pants of his uniform with their white stripe and he saw the man reaching for the gun in his belt. As he moved toward the hedge, the guard switched on a flashlight. Closer and closer he came, swinging a flashlight. Twenty feet from Troy, he stopped.

"Hey, boy. I know you're here," the man said in a soft, creepy voice. "And I know you ain't from here. You little thief."

Slowly, he moved toward Troy, stabbing the flashlight into the hedge, angling it all around. Troy wiggled down deeper into the bush, then froze. The light came his way. He put his head down.

When the light hit him, he shut his eyes and held the football tight, thinking of his mother's words, wishing he'd listened to her when she said he didn't belong there. Wishing he hadn't said his hothead words to Jamie.

Now he was caught. A boy who lied. A boy who snuck out at night. A boy who took something that didn't belong to him. It was *stealing*. He knew the word.

Maybe he really was *that* kind of a kid, and maybe *this* was what was really *meant to be*.

CHAPTER FOUR

BUT THE SECURITY GUARD kept going down the hedge. He called out a few more times, "Get out here, boy. You little thief." Then, after one final snarl, he cursed and got back into the big white truck and drove off.

When the pain in his chest started to fade, Troy stood and brushed off the pine straw and the dirt. He turned the ball in the moonlight and read the words ATLANTA FALCONS. It was official. He swallowed hard and crept out onto the street. He had no idea where he was.

The moon.

He'd seen it shining through his bedroom window. He found it now and went the other way as best he could, chasing his own shadow. Sooner or later, with the moon to his back, he had to find the wall. And he did.

His hands touched the cool surface. He put his cheek against it and looked down its length, straining for something he recognized. He walked one way for a long time. Panic began to rise up in his chest. That's when he heard a whistle. A whistle, clear and keen, like when you call a dog. A whistle like Tate McGreer.

He'd been going the wrong way, but now he doubled back, past where he had started, until finally he found the hole. His friends were waiting for him.

He squeezed through and held the football high, rolling it with his fingers so they could see where "Atlanta Falcons" was stamped into the leather.

"You're bleeding," Tate said, touching his arm.

"It's okay," Troy said, swatting at a mosquito.

Nathan asked what happened, and as the three of them walked back to the railroad tracks, he told them about the security guard.

"I heard that truck racing after you like a crazy man," Nathan said. The whites of his eyes glowed in the moonlight.

Troy shivered, then yawned.

"Well," he said, looking down the tracks in the direction of the apartment complex, then up ahead at the thick pines that surrounded his own home.

"You did it," Tate said, patting his shoulder.

"Here," Troy said, handing her the ball.

"What?" she said, rolling it in her hands.

"That whistle saved me. I'd still be in there," he said.

"No," Tate said, shaking her head and handing back the ball. "I can't."

"You helped," Troy said, pushing it at her.

"No, Troy, I can't."

"I mean it. Here. You can be the one to shove it in Jamie's face, the way he always pulls your ponytail."

But Tate wouldn't take the ball. She stood looking down at her feet, nudging a rock with her toe. Nathan, too, was looking down.

"There were footballs all over the yard," Troy said, his voice sounding small next to the song of the crickets. "He's not going to miss this one."

"Okay, Troy," Nathan said, holding out his hand for Troy to slap him five. "I gotta go. Good job."

Troy gave him five.

"Yeah, good job," Tate said. She slapped hands with Troy, too, then the two friends turned and started down the tracks.

Troy looked at the ball, running his fingers over the "Atlanta Falcons" imprint.

"Hmmph," he said, tucked the ball under his arm, and marched home, thinking about the look he was going to see on Jamie Renfro's face. Jamie's dad might be the big shot with a junior league football team, but that was nothing compared to being connected to a real NFL team.

When he saw his own face in the mirror, he gasped and winced at the same time. He examined his arms and legs under the light. Scratches everywhere, dried dribbles of blood. Pink welts. Too many to hide. His mother would know he'd been out. He would be grounded. He might even be sent off to military school. That subject came up whenever he was unruly. His mom said boys sometimes needed that kind of discipline.

He looked back into the mirror at his own green eyes, the eyes he thought he got from his mother. But sometimes he looked at those eyes staring back at him and wondered if they really were his mother's eyes, the eyes of a good kid. Because maybe they were the eyes of his father. The eyes of a person who'd leave his family and never return.

Troy knew how he could get away with having scratches all over him. The answer came to him without even trying. It was kind of like the gift his friends said he had with football, but this gift was nothing to be proud of.

He would have to lie.

CHAPTER FIVE

BECAUSE HE DIDN'T FEEL so good about tricking his mom, it took a while for Troy to get to sleep. When the alarm clock went off in the morning, though, he jumped out of bed before she could hear it. He stuffed the ball deep into his football equipment bag and hurried out the back door before his mother woke up.

He stayed outside for a while, sitting on the train tracks, listening to a pack of blue jays call the day to life and watching the sun's rays as they began to glint through the trees. It was going to be a hot one. He'd wear eye black for the game, even though he might not get in for a single play. The air got warm and the tar in the railroad ties began to cook and bleed, and then he smelled something else. He got up and followed it all the way to his house.

When he walked through the screen door, he heard the spatter of eggs frying and he inhaled the rich scent of bacon. His mom turned his way from the stove with a spatula in her hand.

"Troy White! What happened?" she said, setting the spatula down and walking over to touch the scratches on his face.

Troy shrugged. "Chasing a snake."

"A snake?"

"For science, Mom. He got into the thick stuff. Just a garter."

"My God, you've got cuts all over you. You've got a football game. I don't want those things in the house."

"I'm fine, Mom," he said, pulling away. "And you don't have to worry about the game unless Jamie Renfro breaks his leg, which I wish he would."

"Troy," she said, frowning. "We don't wish other people ill. Get clean. Your eggs are ready."

"Okay, Mom," he said.

When his mom dropped him off at the game, Troy searched the sidelines for Jamie Renfro. He was standing in a loose circle with a couple of his buddies, bloodying each other's knuckles in a vicious game of slaps. Troy hovered behind them, waiting for Jamie to get a particularly hard penalty smack on the back of his hands after pulling away too soon. He was shaking the sting away when Troy handed him the ball and waited.

The other boys crowded in to see. Jamie glared at Troy, then turned the ball over and over, scowling and acting like it wasn't real. Then he shrugged and flipped it back at Troy.

"My dad says this ball's too big," he said. "We have to use a youth league ball. But you can play with it. On the bench."

Jamie's dad blew the whistle and shouted to his team that it was time for warm-ups. The starting offensive players jogged out onto the field and huddled up, and Jamie sauntered over, snapping his chinstrap.

Troy looked at the ball and suddenly didn't feel as good as he imagined he would, realizing that he would have traded a hundred Falcons footballs to be the one walking out to that huddle, and a hundred more to have a dad who coached the team. But, after everything he'd been through, he was going to get as much out of the Falcons football as he could. So, during the game, whenever Jamie came off the field, Troy made a point to spin it into the air and catch it with a thump, caressing it like a championship trophy. A couple of times he was sure he caught Jamie looking.

As the game unfolded, he fought back the urge to tell Jamie's father how to win. Even though he didn't like the man, Troy wanted Coach Renfro to know that he had a special gift. The Roswell Raiders safeties, who should have been worried about a deep pass, were crowding the line of scrimmage. The linebackers were playing too close to the line as well, all of them focused too much on stopping the Tigers' running back, and not paying any attention to the wide receivers.

Troy knew Jamie's father should have the offense fake the run and have both wide receivers go deep. One of them was certain to be wide open for a touchdown. But Troy knew Jamie's dad didn't like hearing what Troy had to say. He was a coach who believed in yelling, not strategy. So the Tigers kept running the ball, getting stuffed by the safeties, and every so often having Jamie throw short little wobbly passes that people, more times than not, couldn't catch. The Raiders beat them 42–10.

After shaking hands with the Raiders and gathering around with the rest of the team to get yelled at some more by Jamie's dad, Troy tucked the Falcons football back deep into his equipment bag and walked slowly toward his mom. She rubbed his hair and told him not to worry. You can't win them all. Troy looked up at her with damp eyes and opened his mouth to speak.

"What, Troy?" she asked, looking at him with those kind green eyes. She was pretty, even though she was his mom and even though she rarely wore makeup.

Troy wanted to tell her about the safeties playing too close to the line, wanted to tell her that he was a better quarterback than Jamie and the only reason he didn't play was that he didn't have a dad. But his mom didn't like to talk about Troy's dad, a man Troy never knew, and Troy loved his mom a lot, so he said, "Thanks for coming, Mom."

They stopped at Krispy Kreme on the way home for a box of glazed donuts. On the corner where their dirt driveway butted into Route 141, the same old man who was there beside the highway every Saturday morning stood mixing his black pot full of boiled peanuts. Troy's mom pulled over, and he groaned.

"Who would eat those things?" he said.

She smiled at him, patted his leg, and as she got out of the car she said, "Random acts of kindness."

"Hello, Tessa, my beauty," the old man said, grinning at her with a wrinkled and toothless smile. He tipped his faded red cap and hurried back to his steaming pot, spooning mushy peanuts into a rolled cone of newspaper.

Troy's mom took two dollars out of her purse and handed them to the old man. The money quickly disappeared into the front pocket of his overalls, and he handed her the peanuts. Troy turned his head away for a moment and made a face.

"When I franchise these ole peanuts," the old man said, looking into the blue sky above the trees and sweeping his hand, "I'll put your face on a billboard. I'll fly you around on a private jet, my gal, and put you on a TV commercial. That's where you belong, billboards and TV commercials."

Troy's mom touched the old man's shoulder and told him she was counting on it. As they drove down the twisty dirt driveway toward the house, Troy slumped in his seat. It was hot enough now to roast a peanut without a pot. As they walked into their little house, he was thinking about hiking down to the river that afternoon with Nathan and Tate.

That's when the phone rang.

That's when his mom found out she got the job with the Atlanta Falcons.

That's when their whole world got turned upside down.

CHAPTER SIX

ON TUESDAY MORNING, THE day after Labor Day, when Troy saw his mom ready for work, all he could say was "Wow."

His mom's face went pink. She turned around for him, heels clicking the floor, the hem of her blue blazer spinning and floating in the air, and her silk blouse billowing even after she stood still. Troy was used to her dull-brown UPS uniform. The cap that hid her long brown hair. The stiff shorts and brown socks that made her legs look so thin. Now she looked like one of the women he saw on the covers of her magazines.

"Okay," she said, letting her hands fall. "Get your backpack. Here's your lunch."

She was going to drop Troy off at school on her way

25

to work. When she worked at UPS, she had to leave before the school opened and Troy had to walk up their dirt drive to Route 141 and wait for the bus. He liked getting out of his mom's new pale green VW bug and hoped his friends saw just how important she looked, her hair down and dressed for her job with the Atlanta Falcons.

No one did notice, but that didn't keep Troy from getting detention for drawing a falcon on his desk in social studies. While his teachers droned on about math and science, he imagined his mom standing with Michael Vick and maybe even Seth Halloway. He could see them listening to what she told them. He could see their serious faces, their hands on their chins, as she shared her wisdom about how to behave in their interviews with reporters.

The only thing that broke his smile was Jamie Renfro at lunch. Troy was explaining how closely his mom would be working with the Falcons players when he noticed that the friends at his lunch table were staring behind him. Troy turned around and saw Jamie with his arms crossed. He wore a sneer on his face and a blinding white Cowboys jersey. Number 81. Terrell Owens, T.O.

"Too bad your team's gonna get pounded on Sunday," he said, his breath reeking from Doritos.

Jamie didn't always live in Atlanta. He moved there when he was ten years old. Before that, his dad worked in Dallas, so he and his dad were Cowboys fans. The Falcons' opening game was that coming Sunday. They were playing the Cowboys.

"Wanna bet?" Troy said.

"Sure. If that crummy team of your mom's wins, I'll give you my White Shoes ball, and when they lose, you can give me that football your mom stole," Jamie said, laughing.

Troy felt his face go hot. He stood up so fast that the legs of his chair made a squeaking sound on the floor.

"My mom didn't steal anything," Troy said, glaring up at Jamie, his hands balled into fists.

Mr. Squires, the lunch monitor, was making his way toward them through the tables. He raised his voice and said, "Hey, you two."

"Bet me, then," Jamie said, holding out his hand and showing that mean smile of his.

Troy slapped his hand into Jamie's, gripping it as hard as he could. Jamie squeezed back, and his smile got even meaner.

"Hey," Mr. Squires said.

Jamie let go and went back to his seat. When Troy sat back down, none of the guys would look at him. Everyone knew that the Falcons were seven-point underdogs.

On the bus ride home, Troy, Nathan, and Tate agreed to drop off their things at home and meet on the tracks.

Troy got there first. As he waited for his friends to make their way down the tracks, he walked back and forth, balancing on the rail. The Falcons football was under his arm.

"I thought we were trading cards," Nathan said when they arrived. He shook the shoe box he held in front of him.

"We are," Troy said, holding up the ball. "I gotta do this first. I'm putting it back."

"You wanna unload the hot goods," Nathan said.

"It's not *stolen*," Troy said, scowling. "I borrowed it."

"What about your bet?" Tate asked. "If you lose, you have to give it to Jamie."

"My mom will get me another ball," Troy said.

"You wanna wait until dark?" Nathan asked.

"I just want to get it done," Troy said. "Sneak through the bushes and throw it back onto his lawn."

Tate twirled the end of her ponytail and Nathan nodded. They followed him down the other side of the tracks toward the wall. As they got close, Troy held up his hand and his friends stopped.

"Shh," he said, tilting his head.

"What?" Tate said in a hushed voice.

"I don't know," Troy said. "Something's different. I just feel it."

They crouched down in the weeds, and Troy crept toward the hole. When he parted the grass at the edge of the tree line, he saw what had happened. The hole in the wall had been filled in with concrete. He sniffed the air and could smell it. Troy looked up and down the length of the wall. There was no one in sight, and he eased across the open space.

The concrete that had oozed through was damp, but already hard like the frosting on a week-old cake. He ran his fingers over the rough surface until he realized his friends were beside him. He slammed the football against the damp concrete and turned away, trudging back toward the tracks. By the time they reached his house, sweat was streaming down their faces.

Troy took the ball and stuffed it back into the bottom of his equipment bag. After three big glasses of cold grape juice, they pushed the coffee table tight to the couch and spread their cards out on the living room rug. Troy started the trade, giving up two Tampa Bay defensive linemen for the Falcons safety Tate was reluctant to part with. Then he gave Nathan three Giants offensive linemen for the Falcons tight end.

Tate looked over at Nathan with a gleam in her eye and tried to bite back her grin.

"Man, you love those Falcons all of a sudden, huh?" she said, looking at Troy and staring pointedly at the special blue binder he used for storing his very best cards. "Like you'd trade anything to get the whole team, huh?"

Troy looked down at the cards in his shoe box and

raised his eyebrows, shrugging. Tate made him give up Brett Favre and Marvin Harrison for the Falcons kicker.

"Nice friend you are," he said, glaring at her as he slipped the cards out of his binder.

"What?" she said, holding her hands out and up. "I like kickers. I'm a kicker."

Nathan insisted he was quite fond of the Falcons starting right tackle and wouldn't take anything less than Brian Urlacher and Simeon Rice in return. By the time Tate and Nathan had to go for dinner, Troy had given away most of his good cards. He didn't care, though. He had the entire Falcons starting lineup carefully arranged in the blue binder.

"When they win the Super Bowl, you guys won't laugh," Troy said. "They take everyone when they go to the Super Bowl. That means my mom. I'll probably get to go, and I'll get all these signed. Imagine what that'll be worth?"

On the way out the door, Tate stopped and fished into her shoe box. She handed him back Brett Favre, smiled, and gave him a little salute.

"I do like kickers, but Marvin Harrison was enough."

"You're okay," he said, winking. "For a girl."

"Hey," she said, and they all laughed.

Troy watched them through the screen door as they disappeared into the pines. He went and dug through his room, cleaning out anything that had something to do with another team. It meant the books on his shelf had to stand on their own without the help of his New England Patriots bookends. Even his Kurt Warner bobblehead went into the box of non-Falcons things.

He carried the box out of his room with two hands and hoisted it up onto the top shelf of the hall closet. As he climbed down, he heard the VW pull into the bare spot out front. He ran to the front door and yanked open the screen, meeting his mom on the porch. He threw his arms around her, hugging her tight.

"Wow," she said.

He stared up at her and asked, "Did you get it?"

She put her arm around him, squeezing him as they went through the door. "Not yet."

"Aw, Mom."

"Troy," she said, holding up a finger.

"I know," he said.

"But I got this," she said, digging into her purse and holding out a big red card coated in plastic.

Troy took it, asking what it was and turning it over in his hands. Two words in bold print stood out: ALL ACCESS.

"You want to go to the game Sunday?" she asked.

"The Cowboys game? Mom, this isn't a ticket."

"It's better," she said.

"Better?"

"It's a field pass," she said. "I met the owner, Mr. Langan. His son was at practice, and he and I got to talking about kids. I told him I had a son, too, crazy for football. Well, when he asked if you'd ever been to a Falcons game, I had to tell him the truth. And he gave me the pass."

Troy turned it over a few more times and said, "This gets me into the Dome?"

"It gets you in and lets you go anywhere you want to go."

"Mom?"

"Anywhere. With me, but that shouldn't be too bad."

"The locker room?" he asked.

"Anywhere," she said.

"The field?"

"Anywhere."

CHAPTER SEVEN

HIS MOM HAD A parking pass for the garage where the players' cars were. Big, shiny machines, glinting with chrome. Mercedes SUVs and sedans. Cadillac Escalades. Lexus coupes. Porsche convertibles. BMW roadsters. And out of them stepped men so big that Troy had to blink. Men with hands the size of holiday hams. Heads like buckets. Legs like tree trunks.

Some were dressed in jeans and polo shirts and wore only wedding bands or no jewelry at all. Others wore fancy suits with colorful ties and alligator shoes to match. Their watches sparkled with hundreds of diamonds, as did the pendants hanging from their necks like Olympic medals, and their rings looked like Christmas tree ornaments.

Troy felt his mom walking beside him as they went

through the garage and in the side door of the Dome, where they showed the guard at the desk their passes. Players flowed by, silent, with grim faces, on their way to the locker room. Mike Vick, the Falcons' famous quarterback, walked in. He looked the same as he did on the Nike billboards. The same as he did in all those commercials.

Troy felt his mouth fall open. He felt his mom's hand on his arm. She tightened her grip. Troy stared and Mike looked at him, right at him. A white smile lit up the quarterback's face, and he pressed his fist to Troy's shoulder the way his gramps sometimes did.

"Hey, my man," he said, and went on past.

Troy was numb.

After a minute, he realized his mom was tugging at him. He looked up at her and grinned. Troy met his mom's boss, a smiling woman named Cecilia Fetters who carried a walkie-talkie and a clipboard.

"Just keep an eye on the handheld cameras," Cecilia said to his mom, handing her a walkie-talkie. "They like to get inside the bench area. Tell them to leave if they do. Don't be nice about it, either. I know I don't know you that well, but I can tell, if anything, you're too nice. Call me if you have any problems."

Then they were out on the sideline. Except for a handful of security people and ushers, the stands were empty. There were players scattered around on the field, stretching, tossing footballs back and forth, or just standing in small bunches, their voices floating up into the vast empty space. Most of them wore their football pants and shoes with sleeveless T-shirts. Their helmets and shoulder pads were still in the locker room.

One tall player, dressed all in black in skintight pants and a T-shirt, was jogging around the edge of the field. Troy saw him cross the goal line and head up the Falcons' sideline. As he got closer, Troy saw muscles on muscles. All the players were big and built well, but this one looked like a cartoon action figure, with a narrow waist and shoulders and arms as big as cannonballs. Troy moved closer and saw his face and felt a chill.

It was Terrell Owens, the Cowboys' brazen, loudmouthed star receiver. The man who played in the Super Bowl with an unhealed broken leg. The man whose jersey Jamie Renfro loved to wear. Owens's mouth was set in a frown and the lids of his eyes were half shut. He went right past Troy without looking.

Someone put his finger in Troy's back and said, "Hey. Let me see your pass."

Troy held out the red card that his mom had attached to his belt loop and looked up at a man in a yellow windbreaker that said SECURITY. The man examined the pass, then pointed at a broken yellow line that looked like the white one you'd see in the middle of the road.

"You stay behind the yellow line," he said. "You can't go inside that. Players and staff only."

The broken yellow line was ten feet outside the broad white border of the field, and it made a jog around the hundred-foot area where the players' benches were.

Troy jumped back outside the yellow line and said he was sorry. His mom was behind the rectangular bench area, talking to a man in a suit. Troy went and stood next to her, careful to keep well outside of the yellow line.

As the game drew nearer, more and more people crowded into the sideline area outside the yellow line. The stands began to fill with people dressed in red and black, the Falcons' colors. About forty-five minutes before kickoff, the players drifted back into the tunnels that led to their team locker rooms, then came out all together in their uniforms for their official warm-up. TV cameramen and photographers with two-foot lenses jostled each other to get pictures of the stars. Troy kept close to his mom, and every so often he would push through the crowd to get a glimpse of the field and the monstrous players. Then the teams went in and security guards swept the sidelines, telling almost everyone to leave.

When a thick-shouldered guard asked to see his and his mom's pass, Troy crossed his arms and pretended to be searching for someone in the crowd. His mom explained that she was the new PR assistant. The guard turned Troy's pass over and narrowed his eyes.

"Yeah, but he can't stay," the guard said in a rumbling voice, letting go of the pass and nodding at Troy.

"I'm with the public relations department for the *team*," his mom said. "He's my son."

"I don't care who you are, lady," the guard said. "These passes are only for people working.

"The kid has to leave."

CHAPTER EIGHT

"MR. LANGAN GAVE ME these passes personally," Troy's mom said. Her mouth was a flat line and her chin was tilted up at the hefty guard.

"Mr. Langan?" the guard said, looking around and then back at his mom. "He did?"

"Ask him if you like," his mom said. "What's your name?"

"No, it's okay," the guard said, holding out his hands, palms down. "Just keep him behind the yellow, okay?"

The guard walked away, and Troy grinned up at his mom. She raised her eyebrows at him, just for a moment, then dropped them.

"Way to go, Tessa," Troy said, slow-punching her arm.

"Tessa?"

"That's what your friends call you," he said, grinning even wider.

She shook her head, trying to hold back a smile before she turned toward the field for the player introductions.

The Falcons' starting offense ran out through the tunnel, one by one, as their names were called. Fireworks exploded and smoke filled the inside of the Dome. The crowd roared. Troy covered his ears. When the Cowboys were announced, there was only some scattered applause. Drew Bledsoe, their quarterback, got some cheers. But when Terrell Owens ran out through the goalpost, the Dome erupted in loud boos.

Because his mom had to be near the bench during the game, she and Troy stood directly behind where the players sat. They were outside the yellow line, but Troy could still hear the players talking to one another and their coaches, and he could smell the sweat that darkened their jerseys. The game started off slow, with both teams' offenses sputtering and then punting the ball back and forth. At the end of the first quarter, no points had been scored.

Troy's eyes were glued to the field. He paid closest attention to each team's offensive strategy. He saw what the Falcons were doing with Mike Vick. He kept handing the ball off to the running back on the right side, and Troy knew that would open up a bootleg play.

Soon, the whole offense would make it look like it was another run to the right, but Vick would keep the ball instead of handing it off and run the opposite direction, all alone, free to either make a long run or a long pass.

With six minutes to go before the end of the half, they did it. Vick sprinted to his left, wide open. The defense closed in on him, and at the last instant he let the ball fly, striking his wide receiver in the end zone. Touchdown. The place went nuts.

The Cowboys had a long runback after the kickoff. It wasn't enough for a touchdown, but it put them almost close enough to try a field goal. In the Cowboys' huddle, Troy saw the quarterback say something to the running back, Julius Jones, who flexed his hands. He watched the formation and muttered to himself that they were going to run a sweep to the left. They did.

He looked at the marker. Second and five.

"Short pass to Jones," he said to himself under his breath. "Probably an angle route."

It was an angle route.

The running back ran a pattern that looked like a V tipped on its side and caught the ball for what looked like a five-yard gain. It would have been, too, except for Seth Halloway. Seth must have anticipated the angle route as well, because as soon as the ball touched the running back's hands, Seth lowered his shoulder and exploded up through the offensive player, knocking him into the air and jarring the ball loose to fall incomplete onto the turf.

Troy heard the crunch of pads and the huff of air leaving Jones's body. A current of excitement ran through him when he saw Seth's grin and heard him screaming in celebration with the teammates who swarmed him. Troy pumped his fist in the air and screamed along with him, nearly jumping out of his shoes. Some of the players on the bench swung their sweaty heads around, pointed at him, and grinned, nodding their heads as if they liked his enthusiasm. His mom put her hand on his shoulder.

"Draw," Troy said, looking up at his mom. "They'll run the play right at Seth."

They did. The quarterback dropped back, faking a pass, then handed it to the running back, who shot up through the line. Seth was waiting, though, and he dumped the runner on his back a yard short of the first down with a thud that made Troy wince. The crowd roared the old player's name: "Seth. Seth. Seth."

They loved him. He was a hero, a great player, but a great guy, too. He was the guy who handed out toys to homeless kids at Christmas and who dished out soup to street people at the downtown shelters on Tuesday evenings, his day off. Troy loved him for that, but he loved him just as much for his big hits. As Seth came off the field, he raised his arms like lightning rods. By the look in Seth's eyes, Troy suspected that the current of seventy thousand people was flowing right through him.

"Wow, honey," his mom said. "Good guess."

He opened his mouth to tell her that it wasn't a guess, that he somehow just knew. Today, he felt it stronger than he ever had before. Maybe it was because he was right there, on the sideline, seeing it, hearing it, smelling it, living it. The gift inside him felt like a lamp with its shade suddenly pulled off. He wanted to tell his mom that he could help their team win.

Instead, he smiled and shrugged.

The Cowboys kicked a field goal and the half ended with the Falcons on top 7–3. Troy thought about Jamie's NFL football, the one signed by White Shoes Johnson. It would be sweet to get it, but he knew a lot could happen with a half still to play.

Halftime seemed to take forever, but after the teams came out, Troy began calling the plays to himself. He was right every time. The Falcons marched ninety yards, and on third and one from the one-yard line, Troy knew Vick was going to run that bootleg again. No! He had to tell someone. Troy knew the Cowboys' defense would be ready. He just knew it! A reverse by the Falcons, instead of the bootleg, would easily score. A Falcons touchdown would secure the momentum of the game.

He looked around at the players and coaches. Veins

and tendons bulged from their necks. Everyone was staring at the field. The head coach was at the edge of the sideline, surrounded by his offensive assistants and the backup quarterbacks, who were always ready to run in. There was no one Troy could tell. They ran the bootleg and the Cowboys stopped it. The Falcons had to settle for a field goal.

Troy told himself they still had a seven-point lead, but he bit his lip and clenched his hands at his sides, because, just like everyone else, he could feel that the momentum had changed, and he could just see Jamie Renfro's nasty smile.

When the Cowboys came out on the next series, Troy saw what they were doing right away, running a series of pass patterns where the outside receiver ran down the field and broke for the sideline. Soon the Falcons' cornerback would just assume the receiver was going to the outside. The cornerback would jump up and toward the sideline, creating a big open space behind him. That's where the inside slot receiver, Terrell Owens, was going to run in behind him for a touchdown. Troy knew how to stop it, and he was so frantic to tell someone that he began to babble out loud.

His mom gave him a funny look, but she had to leave his side to get a cameraman who was edging around the corner of the bench for a shot of Mike Vick talking to a coach. Troy slipped away and stepped over the yellow line, between the long aluminum benches, past the table of a hundred Gatorade cups. He tapped the arm of a ball boy, a high school kid with the shadow of a mustache, probably a coach's son. The kid looked down at Troy, annoyed.

"Who's the guy calling the defenses?" Troy asked.

"Coach Krock? Over there," the ball boy said, pointing to a crowd of players near the sideline with their helmets under their arms.

Another older boy was standing behind the group, carrying a loop of cable that connected the coach's headset to the scouts and coaches watching from up in the press box. Troy followed the cable, knowing it would take him to the coach. His heart was thumping, because he knew he was just a kid and his instincts told him that most adults would think he was crazy.

He darted into the crowd of players still following the cable, yanked on the coach's shirtsleeve, and yelled, "Wait! You've got to listen!"

As the coach wheeled around, glaring down at him, Troy seemed to see everything at once. The tall, lanky coach's nose was long and his hatchet face was sharp. The Adam's apple in his sunburned neck bobbed, and his dark eyes narrowed at Troy. Coach Krock heaved his right leg around and it clumped on the turf. Troy looked down and saw the plastic ankle and its shiny metal bolt from under the hem of his pants.

Krock grabbed Troy by the collar, ranting, "Who the holy heck is this kid?"

CHAPTER NINE

"COACH, I KNOW WHAT they're going to do!" Troy yelled, struggling to get free.

The coach lost his balance and nearly fell. He yanked Troy to one side, throwing him to the turf and stumbling forward.

"Get this little brat the holy heck out of here!" he shouted, his face scrunching up and turning red as he regained his balance and turned his attention back to the field.

Two security guards in yellow jackets dashed over the yellow lines into the bench area and grabbed Troy under the arms. The players stood holding their helmets and staring at him. Troy felt his eyes begin to fill with those stupid tears. He fought them back as the guards dragged him out of the bench area.

He dug in his heels, gritting his teeth and clenching

his fists as he looked around for his mom. Part of him wanted her to save him. Another part didn't want her to see what he'd done.

"How'd you get this?" one of the guards asked, snapping the field pass off his belt loop and holding it out of his reach.

"My mom," Troy said, still struggling to get free. "She knows Mr. Langan. Let me go."

Their grips only tightened, and they lifted his feet right off the ground, then marched him toward the Falcons' tunnel. They were near the goal line when Troy heard the crowd erupt. Terrell Owens was running down the middle of the field. He faked to the inside. The free safety, Bryan Scott, jumped that way. Then Owens broke back toward the corner of the end zone. The cornerback was up, covering the underneath receiver, who was running the out cut. Owens was wide open and Bledsoe's pass zipped through the air. The Dome broke out into a chorus of boos as Owens held the ball high and strutted around the end zone like a crazy chicken, celebrating his touchdown.

Troy stopped struggling, and the guards set him down and shoved him into the tunnel. Cecilia Fetters, his mom's boss, was waiting there with her walkie-talkie. Her lips were pressed tight. She shook her head in disgust and told the guards to follow her. They took Troy past two state troopers posted outside the door, through the locker room, the training room, and into the back where the public relations department had an office.

"You sit right here, mister," Cecilia said, scowling and pointing at the chair in front of the desk. "We'll deal with this after the game."

She took Troy's pass from the security guard and stuffed it in her own pocket. When she left, she closed the door. Troy shut his eyes and wished he was home on his couch sitting with Tate and Nathan, just watching the game like a normal kid. He could almost imagine it. When he opened his eyes, he looked up and saw the TV hanging from the corner of the ceiling. The volume was down low, but he could hear them announcing the game that was going on outside in the Dome. Troy leaned forward and watched.

The Falcons got two first downs, but the Cowboys' defense seemed to adjust and the Falcons' offense was suddenly having a hard time. It was third and seventeen when Mike Vick ran wildly around the field to bring the Falcons within spitting distance of the goal line. The floor underneath his feet rumbled and Troy could hear the screaming crowd through the walls. He jumped up and cheered, too, then stood with his hands clenched, watching.

Three plays later, the Falcons had to settle for a field goal, but they had the lead now, 13–10. Troy sat back down and put a finger to his mouth, chewing off the end of the nail. He studied the Cowboys' offense,

saw the patterns at once on every pass play, and cal-
culated exactly what it meant without even trying.
Time was running out. The Cowboys had to score a
touchdown, and Troy suddenly knew what they were
waiting for.

If they got the ball near the fifty-yard line, they
were going to run the same play that gave Owens his
touchdown, only this time, his move to the inside
wouldn't be a fake. With the last touchdown play in
his mind, the free safety would be frozen. Owens
would blow right by him. Troy knew the Falcons' free
safety, Bryan Scott, was a smart player, a college aca-
demic all-American and a concert pianist. He might
listen, even to a little kid. Troy's finger shot out of his
mouth and he looked down at his hand. He'd bitten
through the skin.

He got up out of his chair and went to the desk,
looking for a tissue box. There was nothing in sight,
so Troy pulled open a desk drawer. That's when he
saw them, fanned out in a half-circle in the bottom of
the drawer, just like a hand of cards in a poker game.
Red and beautiful with bold black print.

Inside Cecilia Fetters's desk were half a dozen
unused field passes.

CHAPTER TEN

TROY WAS ALREADY IN trouble. It couldn't get worse. But, if he could help the team to win, all might be forgiven. That was a chance worth taking.

He had to hurry. He tied the pass to his belt loop and grabbed the door handle. It was unlocked. He slipped through the training room, passed a dozen padded tables, hot tubs, cold tubs, shelves filled with tape and padding and drugs. The leather and shoe-rubber smell of the locker room filled his nose. He peeked into the cavernous locker room.

It was empty, but Troy knew those two state troopers would still be outside the doors. He moved quickly across the carpet. In the corner of the room another TV hung from the ceiling, the game on low. The Falcons were on their own thirty-yard line. Mike Vick dropped back for a pass but was tackled before he could throw it, sacked for a twelve-yard loss. Less than four minutes remained in the game.

A rattling noise made him jump and spin around.

Only an ice machine.

When he got to the double doors, he pushed one open just a crack and saw the light blue back of a uniform and the grip of a gun in a black leather holster.

Booing rumbled through the Dome. Something bad for the Falcons. Troy took a breath, held on to the pass, and pushed through the doors. He looked up at the trooper on his left, shrugged, and said, "I had to use the bathroom. See you guys."

He kept going, half expecting to hear them yell for him to stop. But they didn't. Instead of heading for the tunnel he'd just come through, Troy scooted the other way, where they hadn't seen him being dragged in. He held out his pass to the guards at every checkpoint and got all the way to the far tunnel before a guard stopped him. The guard carefully examined the field pass.

"My mom is friends with Mr. Langan," Troy said, grinning at them. "I had to use the bathroom."

"Oh," the guard said.

Troy pushed past and walked out onto the sideline. The fans were on their feet, cheering the Falcons' offense. Third down. Vick dropped back and let the ball fly. Troy held his breath as a perfect spiral cut through the air, right into the hands of Peerless Price.

Price dropped it. In the back of his mind, Troy heard Jamie Renfro laughing. The Falcons would have to punt the ball back to the Cowboys. With the ball in the Cowboys' hands, Troy knew the exact pass pattern they would run to get T.O. open in the end zone.

He didn't have much time. He started to jog toward the Falcons' bench. There were yellow-jacketed guards every ten yards. Troy kept his pass out in front of him for them to see. Bryan Scott was buckling up his chinstrap and heading for the field.

Troy dashed over and grabbed his arm.

"Bryan!" he yelled. "T.O. is going to run the post. He's going to break *inside*, not out. You've got to stay to the inside, please."

Bryan Scott looked down at him in disbelief, then looked around as if to see where Troy had come from. The crowd moaned and roared. The Cowboys brought the punt back to the fifty-yard line.

"It'll look like the same play he scored on the first time," Troy said, backing away now but keeping his eyes on Scott. "They'll do it on the first play. Please."

Then Seth Halloway was there in front of him.

"Who is this kid?" Seth asked.

Bryan shrugged and turned toward the field.

"Crazy kid," Seth said, chuckling, and followed him.

Troy heard Krock's growl an instant before he felt

the iron grip on his shoulder. There was yelling and more hands were on him. He was pushed to the ground, and that's when he heard his mom yelling.

"What's wrong with you!"

She wasn't yelling at Troy, though. She was yelling at Coach Krock.

"Lady, get outta my way," Krock said, pushing past her and clumping toward the field.

This time, Troy let them drag him away without a fight. His mom followed and begged the guards to let him go.

Cecilia Fetters appeared, yelling at the top of her lungs. Police came this time along with security, and a small knot of people surrounded him and his mom, moving them toward the tunnel. On the field, the Cowboys snapped the ball. Troy watched T.O. run down the middle of the field and break to the inside. As if he hadn't heard a word Troy said, Bryan Scott froze, expecting T.O. to break back out.

When Scott realized what had happened, it was too late. T.O. was in the end zone, wide open, catching Bledsoe's arcing pass for a touchdown and doing his crazy chicken dance. The roaring crowd went silent, then started to boo at T.O. The only cheering came from the Cowboys' bench. Troy looked at the scoreboard and saw six points go up for the Cowboys.

He dropped his head, thinking of Jamie Renfro, laughing in his face with that Doritos breath in front of the entire lunchroom. He also thought about the Falcons football his mom hadn't yet been able to get for him.

This time Cecilia Fetters took him past the locker room and right to the door by the players' garage, the same way they'd come in. The people at the desk stared at the crowd escorting them out and the loud voices going back and forth. Troy realized that the raised voices belonged to his mom and her boss. A policeman opened the doors and out they went, he and his mom pushed through while the guards stayed behind.

His mom spun around and told Cecilia Fetters she was totally wrong about her son, no matter how things looked.

"Well, you enjoy him, honey," Cecilia said with her face pinched and her arms waving in the doorway. "He's all yours. And don't neither of you have to worry about coming back here."

She slammed the glass and metal door in their faces, but not before her final words snuck through.

"You're fired!"

CHAPTER ELEVEN

TROY'S MOM GLUED HER eyes to the road. Her hands clenched the wheel and she drove too fast. The little car's engine screamed and the gears crunched as she shifted. Tires squealed around the corners. In the backseat, Troy's head bumped into the window. He watched the back of her head and opened his mouth to talk almost a dozen times. No words came out. Finally, he hung his head and leaned into the curves.

When they slid into the bare spot in front of their house and shuddered to a stop, his mom got out and slammed the door. He watched her disappear through the cloud of red dust, waiting for the front door to slam too before he got out himself. It was a long walk through the woods and down the tracks to the Pine Grove Apartments. Neatly shaped trees grew from beds of flowers edged with pine straw and the side-walks gleamed under the sun.

Troy remembered watching the big yellow earth-moving machines that cleared away the woods for the place when he was only a first-grader. He was excited when he saw that the gray wooden shingles were trimmed with fancy white molding and columns. They made Troy think of the big mansions rich people used to live in down on Jekyll Island, and he thought his new neighbors were sure to be rich too.

When he reached the last unit on the end of the middle building, he rang the bell and Nathan's mom let him in. Nathan was on his couch, watching the four-o'clock NFL game with his dad. The two of them were wearing Chicago Bears caps, and Nathan's dad pushed a half-eaten sandwich and some empty beer cans aside so he could put his feet up on the coffee table. His eyes never left the TV. Troy stood just inside the door and motioned for Nathan to come outside.

"Want to come to the river?" Troy asked.

"Come in and watch with us," Nathan said.

Troy looked down. "Nah."

"How was the game?" Nathan asked.

"They lost."

"I know that, but on the sideline?"

"It was okay."

Nathan's dad jumped up from the couch, shouting and clapping his hands.

"Nathan, touchdown!"

"Come on," Nathan said to him. "I'll get you a soda."

"No, you go," Troy said, and without looking back, he turned and headed for Tate's place.

She answered the door in a white dress. In her long dark hair was a pale blue ribbon.

"Church," she said, shrugging. "Then my uncle came over with his new wife for dinner, so my mom said I had to stay dressed, but I'm almost done with the dishes."

"Can you come to the river?"

"Maybe. Don't you want to watch the Bears game?"

"I hate football," he said, staring into her brown eyes, trying to keep his own from filling up.

"Hang on," she said.

She disappeared for a few minutes, then came back out in a pair of cutoff jeans and a big T-shirt with her bathing suit underneath. She followed him to the tracks.

Troy stood there, looking north. Two lines of steel stretching to the horizon, where they came together like chopsticks that God might use to pluck up an entire train or someone's house.

"What are you doing?" Tate asked.

"Just thinking about where this goes," he said, nudging the steel track with his toe.

"All over the whole country, if you want it to," she said.

"I'm talking about the train to Chicago," he said.

"So?" Tate said.

"Part of me—" he started to say, then stopped.

"Yeah?"

"Nothing," he said.

"You can say it. It's me."

"I think my dad lives there," he said. "I heard my mom talking on the phone once. She thought I was asleep."

Her mouth fell open and she said, "How come you never said anything?"

"Somebody dumps you like garbage, you don't just bring it up. You dream about it like an idiot, like, yeah, I'll just hop on the train someday. Maybe he's waiting for me up there. Right. How stupid is that?"

"It's not stupid," Tate said.

"He used to play football," Troy said. "Big-time football at Auburn. Can you imagine if he coached our team? Not that he would, even if he was here. What kind of guy runs off on his family?"

"Maybe something happened," Tate said quietly.

"I don't want to talk about it," he said, scooping up a stone and tossing it into the woods. "Come on."

They walked side by side along the tracks until they came to the black steel train trestle that spanned the Chattahoochee River—the Hooch. Nearly thirty feet below them the milky green water snaked along.

Instead of taking the dirt path down the bank like

Tate did, Troy kept going, following the tracks out onto the trestle. When he got to the middle, he stopped.

"What're you doing?" Tate asked. She had come back up the path and was walking toward him along the tracks.

His breath was coming short and fast. He felt like he needed to do something crazy, something wild, maybe even something that would get him hurt. Sometimes high school kids would build fires in the woods and drink cans of beer, then jump off the trestle into the Hooch. Everyone heard the story about the kid who jumped off the bridge one time and broke his back on a floating log.

Troy imagined himself laid up in the hospital, getting all kinds of flowers and candy and balloons after breaking a leg and nearly drowning. Then how would his mom feel? She wouldn't care about losing her dumb job with the Falcons. She'd be sorry then.

And his dad?

What if something really bad happened? Some freak thing like the kid who hit the log. Troy stepped to the edge, gripped the steel, and hung out over the river. How would his dad feel when he got the news?

"Troy!" Tate screamed. "You crazy?"

He took a deep breath and jumped. The water came up at him, fast.

CHAPTER TWELVE

IT WAS DARK AND cloudy under the water, and Troy fought, climbing for the surface. When he broke into the air, he gasped and then choked. There was a terrific splash next to him, and by the time he realized what it was, Tate was near. She grabbed him by the collar and started dragging him toward the bank.

"I'm okay," he said, shrugging her off as he swam.

They splashed up into the mud and sat panting. The current had carried them a ways from the trestle, but they could still see it, a black steel skeleton stretching between the dusty trees.

"What were you doing?" Tate said, huffing and scowling at him.

Troy shrugged and looked down at his hands and told her the story of what had happened at the game.

"That's no reason to kill yourself," she said.

"I wasn't killing myself," Troy said. "People do it all the time."

"We don't," she said. "You know it's crazy."

"My mom couldn't even *talk* to me, she was so mad," he said.

"Sometimes people just need to cool down," she said.

"Now I can't even give that football back," he said, looking up at Tate. "I owe that jerk Jamie."

"Well, Seth Halloway isn't going to miss one football."

"He laughed at me, Tate. They all did, everyone on that sideline, but I was right and they lost. Why wouldn't anyone listen?"

"You're a kid."

"I'm going to be thirteen," he said.

"Yeah," she said, "a kid to them."

"I don't even care," he said, standing up and peeling off his wet shirt. "Let them lose. Come on, let's swing from the rope."

"You mean you don't want to jump from the trestle again?" she asked, falling in behind him as he picked his way along the bank back toward their rope tree.

Troy looked up at the trestle. "It seems even higher when you're up there."

Tate took a jackknife out of her pocket and picked up a stick, whittling it as they walked.

"I'd like to cut that Jamie Renfro's hamstring," she said, holding up the blade. "Then you'd be the quarterback and *we'd* win some games."

Troy looked at her. One eyebrow was way up on her forehead and the other was scrunched down over her other eye like some kind of mad pirate. The knife blade glinted in front of her face.

Then both of them started to laugh.

They climbed the bank and unwound the rope from the twisted old tree trunk. Together, they picked up the end of the thick horsehair rope and ran off the edge of the bank, swinging high up into the air nearly ten feet high, hanging there, floating and grinning at each other before they dropped into the river.

Up and down they went, swinging, floating, and falling until they were breathing hard and the shadows were long. They walked dripping down the railroad tracks, and when they were nearly to the path that led through the pines to Troy's house, he said, "I'm done with the Falcons. If they're that stupid, I'm rooting for the Tennessee Titans."

"They barely have any players," Tate said.

"They've got Jeff Fisher for a coach," he said. "They don't need players. He'd listen to someone if they were right, even if they were twelve."

"Okay," Tate said, putting her arm around his shoulders as they walked the rest of the way to his drop-off point. "I'm a Titans fan too."

Troy gave her a squeeze, then jumped down off the railroad bed before turning and looking back up at her.

"You know," he said. "If I was ever gonna have a girlfriend, which I'm not, it'd be you."

She looked down at him.

"Same here," she said, her face turning red. "Which I'm not either."

"I know," Troy said. "I was just saying. Really what I wish is that you were my sister."

"I kind of am anyway, right?" she said.

Troy grinned at her and shrugged and turned for home. As he passed through the pine trees and the warm scent of their sap, the thrill of swinging into the water and Tate's happy face began to fade. Every step brought him closer to the ugly reminder of what had happened at the game. The humiliation of the players and coaches treating him like he was some kind of crazy kid. T.O. scoring a touchdown that could have been stopped. Losing the bet to Jamie Renfro. His mom getting fired. By the time he climbed up onto the porch and swung open the squeaky screen door, he didn't think he could feel any worse.

He was wrong.

His mom stamped out from the kitchen, scowling.

"And where did you get *this*, young man?" she asked, her voice shrieking like the tires of her car on the ride home. "I go to wash your smelly equipment and I find *this*?"

In her hand was the stolen football.

CHAPTER THIRTEEN

EXCEPT FOR THE PART about Nathan and Tate going with him to the hole in the wall, Troy told his mom the truth about what he'd done and why. There were times he had to back up and tell it over because he was sobbing so hard she couldn't understand him. The part that seemed to make her maddest of all was when he told her about Jamie Renfro.

"He didn't believe you were with the Falcons," Troy said, "and I wanted to show him."

"You think it matters what Jamie Renfro thinks of me?" she said, raising her voice to a howl. "You think that's a reason to *steal*?"

His mom paced the living room, yelling wildly about how wrong it was to steal. Her ranting then turned into how he'd ruined her chance at the best job she'd ever had in her whole life. Then to how he probably should be sent to military school. Then she did the worst thing of all: She stood still, looking at him until her breathing slowed, and said she'd never been ashamed to call him her son. Now she was.

"So I'll go live with my father," Troy said, the words coming out of his mouth before he could take them back.

His mother looked like she'd been hit with a board. She stepped across the room and raised her hand, swinging it through the air.

Troy winced, but her hand only slapped the cushion on the couch next to his head. She staggered back, a look of surprise on her face, then straightened herself and tilted her chin up.

"A father is someone who pays the bills and helps you with your homework, Troy," she said. "You don't have a father. I know that hurts. I'm sorry."

She walked out of the house with her head high, but before she got off the porch, a single, miserable sob escaped from her.

Troy ran to his room. He slammed the door and threw himself onto the bed.

"You're all so stupid!" he screamed into his pillow, pounding on it with a fist. He meant the parents, the coaches, and the players. Everyone over the age of thirteen. The Duluth Tigers as well as the Atlanta Falcons. "All I want to do is help them *win*! But no one will give me a *chance*!"

It dawned on him then that a kid without a father wasn't likely to ever get a chance. He tried to let the anger burn so hot that it would snuff out the shame, but it was a losing battle. He tossed and turned for what seemed like hours before, finally, he fell asleep.

The next morning, when his mom nudged him to wake up, there was an instant where it seemed like the whole thing might have been just a dream. Then he heard the cold tone of her voice.

"Come on," she said.

Weak daylight came in through the window. His mom was already dressed up in pants and a blazer. She threw open his closet, yanked a shirt and a pair of dress pants off their hangers, and threw them onto his bed along with a pair of shoes.

"Brush your teeth and put that on," she said, walking out of the room.

The clothes were stiff and the inside seam of the shirt collar scratched his skin. The shoes were tight. When he came out into the kitchen, there was a glass of juice and a bowl of dry cornflakes next to the milk carton.

"Eat," she said, pointing, then turning away to look out the window over the sink while she silently sipped her coffee.

Troy wasn't hungry. His stomach was clenched tight, but he was afraid not to eat. She stood there, watching.

He finished it all, rinsed his dish, and put it in the sink. Without speaking, his mom walked out of the house. He took his backpack off its hook and followed her, climbing into the front seat while she revved the engine. The football was wedged into the space between their seats. He wanted to ask where they were going as they swerved down the dirt driveway, squealing out onto Route 141, but his throat was too tight to speak because he figured he knew.

When they went past the place where they should have turned for his school, Troy sat straighter and looked at the road ahead. Eventually, they got on the main highway and headed north. When she slowed down for the Flowery Branch exit, he stopped praying for a miracle. He knew for sure now that they were heading for the Falcons' training facility, and it made his knotted stomach turn. He remembered being very young and taking a pack of gum from the store. He hadn't even known what stealing was back then, he was that little. He sure knew what it was after his mom dragged him back into the store. She made him give back the gum and apologize to the scowling man behind the counter.

The man behind the counter this time was Seth Halloway, and Troy thought he would rather have their car go off the bridge than make it to the Falcons' facility. The complex was a big brick building with a black iron fence that surrounded everything, including the three grass football fields and a white bubble like an airplane hangar that covered a turf field for indoor practices. There was a guard at the entrance, but when he saw Troy's mom, he waved her in with a smile.

"Must not have heard about your little incident," his mom said bitterly, under her breath, glancing at Troy in the mirror.

They pulled into the circular drive at the main entrance and went inside. There was a guard there, too, who looked at his mom's pass and nodded. She dragged Troy by the wrist into the back and threw open the door to a small office. There was a box of pictures on the desk along with a phone and some books. Troy knew they were the pictures, mostly of him, that she'd taken from the house to hang in her new office.

"This *was* my office," she said, putting the stolen football into the box of pictures and scooping it up under her arm.

Then she dragged him upstairs, where the red carpet was lush and the office doors were trimmed in dark wood. When Cecilia Fetters looked up from her desk and saw them, her face clouded over and she stood up.

"We came to apologize," his mom said. She thrust Troy through the door.

His face was hot and he looked at his shoes and said he was sorry.

"That's very nice," Cecilia said stiffly, coming out

from behind her desk, "but I'm in the middle of something and I'll have to ask you to leave now."

"We kind of need to see Seth Halloway," his mom said, gripping the football and showing it to her. "This is his."

"That's fine," Cecilia said, reaching for the ball. "The players are in meetings already. I'll take that."

"No," his mom said, pulling the ball away and putting it back into the box. "Troy needs to do it himself."

Cecilia's mouth fell open. She stared at Troy's mom and shook her head, huffing out a little laugh.

"I'm sorry you thought this job was a chance for your son to meet the players," she said, "but it's not. It *wasn't*."

"That has nothing to do with it," his mom said.

"Please. Leave."

Troy's mom snatched his hand and down the hall they went. They were almost to the top of the stairs when the head coach and some men in business suits spilled out of a big office looking grim. Troy's mom stopped and looked at the floor, waiting for them to empty out of the hall. When they were gone, she dragged him down the stairs. They were halfway down when a voice came from above.

"Tessa, is this your son?"

They froze and looked up toward the voice. Mr. Langan, the owner, was leaning over the railing dressed in a neat gray suit and wearing a small smile.

"I'm sorry, Mr. Langan," his mom said.

"Well, it was only one game," the owner said with a serious expression. "No one wants to start the season with a loss, but we'll bounce back."

"I meant what happened," his mom said.

Mr. Langan's graying eyebrows moved up, wrinkling his tan forehead.

"What happened?" he asked.

"Well," his mom said. She let go of Troy's hand and walked slowly up the steps. Troy didn't know what to do, so he followed her and looked at his feet while she told the owner the story of him getting kicked out of the Dome. She did it without trying to make any excuses, and when she was done, there was only silence. Finally, Troy looked up at the owner. Mr. Langan's pleasant face lost its expression and he looked down at Troy with sad green eyes.

CHAPTER FOURTEEN

"I'M VERY SORRY," **HIS** mother said in a quiet voice.

"Well," Mr. Langan said, patting her arm. "Kids get excited, don't they? I think Cecilia is right about maybe not having Troy down on the field during the game. I'll take the blame for that. But I tell you what—does he have school?"

"Yes."

"Well, you go take him to school, and by the time you get back, I'll have talked with Cecilia. I'm pretty sure we can find a way to work this out."

His mom said a quiet thank-you and dragged Troy out of the offices like the place was on fire. On the way to the school, his mom looked at him in the mirror and said, "If I get that job back, don't think you're getting away with anything. You're getting punished no matter what. You don't even know how bad."

* * *

Troy spent his morning dodging through the crowded hallways from class to class, keeping a watchful eye out for Jamie. At lunch, he ditched his regular group of friends for a seat with a bunch of brainy kids who always took the table in the back corner. Troy sat with his back to the lunchroom and ate hunched down over his chicken and mashed potatoes with gravy, moving the straw to his mouth without picking up his head.

His straw made a slurping sound at the bottom of his milk when he noticed the guys around him had stopped talking. Troy smelled Doritos. He sighed and closed his eyes for a moment.

"Thought you could hide with these goobers in the corner?"

It was Jamie, and his words rolled into a mean laugh that was automatically imitated by his gang. Troy picked up his tray and turned around to face him like nothing was wrong.

He shrugged and said, "What?"

Jamie put his pointer finger into Troy's chest and said, "Your team sucks and you owe me, that's what."

"Yeah, I know. You know I've got it," Troy said, glancing at Jamie's friends, a tough-looking bunch, each one a frequent visitor to the principal's office. They all wore red Converse sneakers, the old canvas style, with black laces.

"Where?" Jamie asked, folding his arms and frowning.

"I left it at my grandfather's," Troy said, the lie flowing effortlessly from his mouth. "I went over to his house after our game the other day and forgot to bring it home. I'll get it."

"The last goober that welched on me got bumped around in the hallways pretty good," Jamie said, smirking.

"I'm no welcher," Troy said. "You'll get your ball."

He'd seen Jamie and his red-sneaker bunch bullying kids, dumping their books in the halls, tripping them, and poking them in the back with pencils. Troy got ready with his tray, figuring if they tried to get tough with him that at least Jamie was going to get what was left of his mashed potatoes right in the mouth. As if they sensed this, the group parted and Troy walked through them with his tray.

After he got his tray on the conveyor belt, Troy looked around and ducked out the side door.

Troy got to football practice late. So, even though Coach Renfro barked at him and made him run two penalty laps, at least he didn't have to stand around and listen to Jamie. Coach Renfro treated every minute of practice as serious as if it were the final two minutes of the Super Bowl. Once practice began, even Jamie didn't get to chatter or fool around.

After stretching, they went to individual drills. The running backs and quarterbacks worked together on handoffs, then short passes. Troy got to take one turn for every five of Jamie's, but still he was smoother and quicker than the coach's son and the runners never fumbled the handoffs he tucked neatly into their arms.

Jamie's father pretended not to notice, but Troy would catch him looking, especially when they started passing the ball. Whereas Jamie's passes were wobbly and inaccurate, Troy's throws were crisp and precise, hitting the backs right in their hands. When the receivers joined them and the passes got deeper, Troy's throws would whistle through the air. He had the knack for leading his teammates so they didn't have to slow down. They just kept running full speed and the ball would be there.

But after three or four miserable attempts by Jamie to complete the longer passes, his dad blew his whistle to start the team drills. That's when Troy was told to learn by watching.

Halfway through practice, Troy was surprised to see another team arrive in half a dozen cars and vans. They had orange helmets and blue practice jerseys, and after piling out of their vehicles, they regrouped on the sideline of the Tigers' practice field. When Coach Renfro noticed them, he blew his whistle and called everyone in to announce that he'd arranged a scrimmage with the Norcross Knights.

Troy's team cheered. A referee even showed up wearing his stripes, and all the kids and coaches migrated from the dug-up practice field onto the pristine field where the games were played. The thick green grass had just been cut and the air was heavy with its smell. Jamie and a couple of his buddies started talking tough. That's when Troy noticed that Jamie was wheezing just a little at the end of his sentences. Troy stood on the sideline by the bleachers with the rest of the second-string players, watching the Knights beat the stuffing out of his team. He forgot all about the wheezing until Jamie dropped to the ground and began rolling back and forth on the grass.

Coach Renfro ran out onto the field, pulled his son's helmet off, and loosened his shoulder pads. When he found out that Jamie hadn't taken his allergy medicine, his face turned purple and he growled at Jamie. While Coach Renfro and one of his assistant dads helped Jamie off the field, Troy heard Jamie's dad tell the Knights' coach that they couldn't scrimmage anymore.

"You gotta have another quarterback," the Knights' coach said, rumpling his brow.

Troy didn't hesitate. He jammed his helmet on and darted out onto the field, raising his hand like he was in school.

"I can go in, Coach," he said to Jamie's dad as he buckled up his chinstrap. "I'm ready."

"You're ready, huh?" Coach Renfro said with an angry scowl. "You weren't ready when practice started. You weren't even here."

The Knights' coach looked from Troy to Coach

Renfro and said, "Come on, Coach. My guys need the work."

Jamie's dad turned his attention back to Jamie and waved his hand in disgust. "Go, then."

Troy couldn't even feel his feet underneath him. The only other times he'd gotten to run the offense, even in practice, was with the other second-string players, kids who didn't know the plays, or couldn't run or catch, or who stood straight up on the snap of the ball and got knocked over by the defense. Now he'd be with the best athletes their team had. It made a huge difference.

This was his chance.

CHAPTER FIFTEEN

THE SUN WAS ALREADY below the trees and the grass had begun to cool. Troy knew he didn't have much time, so he stepped into the huddle, clapped his hands three times, and said, "Let's go." Nathan, who was the first-string left tackle, extended his hand across the huddle. Troy grinned and shook it, then looked to the sideline, where one of the assistant coaches gave the signal for the offensive play.

It was a simple running play up the middle. Troy called it, broke the huddle, and followed his team to the line. As he put his hands up underneath the center to take the snap, he saw the defense. The linebackers and the strong safety were crowding the line. He knew a run up the middle was the worst thing to do against a defense like that, but he had to show the coach he could do as he was told. He barked out the cadence.

"Down, set, hut one, hut two."

The ball was snapped into his hands. He spun deftly and handed it off to the fullback.

No gain.

The Knights' defense cheered and slapped each other on the back. Troy went back to the huddle with his team. When the assistant coach signaled in another running play, Troy shook his head and gritted his teeth, but did as he was told. He took the snap and handed it off again. Again, the Tigers' runner was thumped right at the line.

It was third down now. On the sideline, Jamie was sitting on the bench with his shoulder pads off, sipping from a bottle of water. Coach Renfro was back now, and he signaled in the next play, another run up the middle. Troy made an appealing gesture, silently begging for something that would help them get the ten yards they needed for a first down. Coach Renfro just stared at him with a frown and folded his arms across his chest.

Troy joined the huddle and knelt down so he could look up into the faces of his teammates.

"They're whipping our butts," Troy said. "Did you hear them laughing? Bust them in the mouth. Give me four seconds and we'll score. Four seconds—can you do it?"

"Yes," Nathan said.

The others blinked and nodded.

Troy turned to Rusty Howell, their skinny wide receiver who was as quick as a hiccup and had the best hands on the team.

"Okay, Rusty," Troy said, "it's on you. Red Right, Thirty-one Dive Play Pass, Zebra Post, on one. Ready—"

"Break!"

Even Troy was surprised at how easily the words for the complex play spilled from his mouth. He jogged to the line, afraid that Coach Renfro would somehow know what he'd done and stop him before he could run the play. He put his hands up under the center and began to call out the snap count, forcing the defense to get into their positions. The free safety, who was the last defender in the middle of the field, drifted deep. He'd be in perfect position to cover Rusty when he ran deep and bent in toward the middle on the Zebra Post. Troy wished there were a way he could change the play. He made a quick hand motion for Rusty to break out toward the sideline instead. But Rusty's eyes were glued to the cornerback in front of him.

It happened in seconds. Troy finished barking out the count, took the snap, faked the handoff, and dropped back into the pocket. A linebacker broke right through the offensive line and dove at Troy. He ducked and spun, then set his feet.

More defenders were fighting through the line, coming at Troy. Rusty was streaking up the field. The free safety didn't bite on the run action. He stayed deep. If Troy threw it now, the safety could intercept it. If he waited, Rusty would be so far down field, Troy didn't know if he could reach him.

The defense was coming, but Troy had to wait. If the pass was going to make it that far, he needed to stoke his arm with blinding anger. So he thought of his father, the man who abandoned him. When Rusty got open, Troy used his fury to launch the ball. It left his hand, a perfect spiral, arcing up through the air, and then he got hit. Stars exploded behind his eyes and everything was dark.

Troy pushed the big defensive lineman off him and struggled to his feet. The free safety was on his knees. Rusty was in the end zone holding the ball up high.

Touchdown.

Troy followed the rest of the offense into the end zone to swamp Rusty. When he got there, they swamped him too. The kids were laughing and slapping high fives until Coach Renfro ran over into their midst and started grabbing guys by the face masks and telling them to calm down.

"Hey!" he screamed. "Get over to the sideline! Troy, you give me ten laps around the field! You don't change my plays! Who the heck do you think you are?"

Troy's face fell. He bit down hard on his mouthpiece and started to jog off the field. As he passed the Knights' head coach, the man said, "Whale of a pass, son. Thirty-eight yards in the air. That was one heck of a pass."

By the time Troy finished his penalty laps, the scrimmage was over.

CHAPTER SIXTEEN

TROY HAD NEVER REALLY been grounded before. Maybe his mom had kept him home for an afternoon or even a whole day once when he left his new bike out in the rain. This was the real thing, though. A solid week of nothing but school, homework, and chores. No friends. No TV. No Xbox. He thanked God for books. What he was having a hard time being thankful for were meals.

His mom put the football he'd taken in the middle of the kitchen table, reminding him that he was not only a liar and a thief but also a welcher, because he owed that ball to Jamie.

"When I get myself back on solid ground at work," she told him that first night, planting the ball between the salt and pepper shakers and the napkin holder, "you'll take this back to Seth Halloway yourself. In the meantime, you can think about it."

Except for the way that the football made it hard to swallow his food, the week actually went along okay. His mom started forgetting to be mad, and he caught her smiling at him and even humming to herself as she pored over the newspapers she would bring home from work, snipping out articles on the Falcons with the same scissors she used to mend the holes in his football pants.

At dinner on Friday night, Troy's mom set down her fork and reached for the football. His insides got tight.

She tossed it to him across the table and said, "Seth Halloway's coming by tomorrow after the team photo. You better take this and think about what you're going to say."

Troy sat there with his head down, turning the ball over slowly in his hands while she picked up the dishes.

"I'm going to watch the news," she said, wiping her hands on a towel and moving into the living room, turning on the TV. "You get to your room."

He went, setting the football on his dresser, kicking back on his bed, and reading *Hoot*. A little after nine, she tapped on his door and came in. She sat on the edge of his bed and touched his hair.

"You can't take things, Troy," she said. "You can't steal."

"There were footballs all over the lawn, like a million of them."

"But that doesn't matter."

"I'm sure he loses them in the bushes."

"This one didn't get lost," she said, then paused for a minute, staring at the window screen.

Troy's eyes went back to his book and he pretended to read.

She sighed and said, "You mentioned your father."

Troy looked up at her. She was frowning and her eyes had a faraway look.

"He couldn't own up to his responsibilities," she said. "He moved to Chicago before you were even born. I won't let you be like that, Troy."

"I always own up," Troy said, scowling and raising his chin at her.

He shut his book and rolled on his side, turning out the light. His back was to her. He listened to her stand up and walk to the door. Then she came back in and kissed the back of his head.

"I love you," she said.

Then she was gone.

Somewhere in the night, Troy woke to the sound of the train. He looked at the red numbers on his clock. Midnight. Tate called it the midnight express. One of the freight trains to Chicago. Troy shut his eyes and tried not to think about it. His mom's words rang out in his mind: *You don't have a father.* The train wailed in the distance. Running north. Running away, to

Chicago. After a time, even though Troy knew it was gone, he kept hearing its sound on the edge of his mind.

When he got up, the sun was already well up and his room was warm. His mom was long gone. Troy ate a bowl of cereal and looked at the list of chores on the counter. He filled five big bushel baskets with pinecones they'd need for starting fires in the winter. He stacked the baskets in the shed and was trying to wash the sticky sap off his fingers with the garden hose when he heard the growl of a truck.

A big yellow H2, shrouded in dust, rumbled into sight and stopped. The engine went dead and the door swung open. Troy saw a man's black cowboy boots and jeans. The door slammed shut, and he gulped. Seth Halloway stood staring across the dirt at him, wearing an angry scowl.

CHAPTER SEVENTEEN

TROY DROPPED THE HOSE and stood up, barely noticing the water soaking through his sneakers.

"Yeah?" Seth said, stepping toward him. "And you got something that belongs to me, your mom told me?"

Troy kept his eyes on the thick linebacker and walked sideways toward the front door. Seth had brown eyes and hair that was long enough to flip up on the outside of his helmet when he played. His nose was slightly crooked and looked as if someone had pushed the tip of it flat and it never came back out. His tight black T-shirt showed a chest and arms that were chiseled with muscle. Seth even had muscles in his face. Troy could see them rippling in his cheeks.

When he reached the porch, Troy turned and scrambled inside. Snatching the ball off his dresser, he dashed back out onto the porch, breathless. A blue jay scolded from up in a tree, and Seth had his eyes shaded against the sun, searching for the bird.

When Seth took the ball, he turned it over in his hands as if to see what damage Troy had done.

"Where is your mom, anyway?" Seth asked, fixing him with a dark, unblinking eye while the other seemed to squint.

"Work," Troy said.

Seth nodded and said, "I must have beat her back here. I hope she isn't waiting for me at the facility. Anyway, you took this, huh?"

Troy nodded.

"How'd you get in?"

"There was a hole in the wall, but they filled it up," Troy said.

"So I don't have to worry about you kids stealing my hubcaps?"

"I went to bring it back," Troy said, "honest. That's when I found out the hole was filled. Then my mom found the ball and . . . It wasn't right to take it anyway."

"Well," Seth said, looking down at the ball, "I appreciate you returning it. I tell you what."

He spun the ball up in the air and Troy caught it. Seth's eyes glittered, and he pressed his lips together as if holding back a grin.

"You tell me how you knew T.O. was gonna break inside instead of outside on that touchdown play last Sunday," Seth said, "and you can keep the ball."

Troy gripped the ball so tight the laces cut into his skin.

"I just know," he said.

Seth let his grin loose and said, "Lucky guess. Okay. You can still keep it."

"No," Troy said, "I *know*."

Seth cocked his head and said, "You know."

"There's patterns," Troy said. "Like . . . like the weatherman on TV. Like rain coming one way and cold air coming another and he knows it's gonna snow."

"You mean tendencies," Seth said. "I know all about tendencies. We get computer breakdowns. Gives us a percentage of the kind of plays teams like to run depending on which players are in the game, the formation, the field position. I know tendencies better than anyone, kid. Trust me."

"That too," Troy said, glad Seth understood part of it. "But it's more. There are patterns."

"You mean like when they draw up a play in the playbook with Xs and Os and arrows going all over the place?" Seth asked.

"Kind of," Troy said.

"And you just see those lines and stuff when you watch a football game?"

"I see it all," Troy said. "At the same time. It's hard to explain. I guess it's like ESP or something."

"In any game?" Seth asked, narrowing his eyes and tilting his head in doubt. "You just see it."

Troy nodded his head. The jay cawed and took off, flying in a blur of black and blue and white.

Seth looked at his watch. "The Georgia Tech game is on in five minutes. You gonna tell me what happens in that?"

"If we watch."

Troy walked into the house and Seth followed, sitting down on the couch next to him as he clicked on the TV. The announcers were just wrapping up their commentary and a commercial came on.

"You want a soda?" Troy asked.

"Sure," Seth said.

Troy got two bottles from the fridge, knowing his mom wouldn't mind him being nice to a guest, especially Seth Halloway. The phone stared at him from the wall and he set the sodas down and called Tate, whispering into the phone that Seth Halloway was on his couch and that she should grab Nathan and come over quick to get his autograph.

"Don't say I called," he said before hanging up. "Pretend you're just stopping by."

"With my football?" she said.

"Like we're gonna practice."

"You're grounded till tomorrow," she said. "No friends, I thought."

"My mom loves you. She's not gonna be mad about you getting an autograph. It's *Seth Halloway*."

Troy went back into the living room and handed Seth

his soda before sitting down. Georgia Tech received the ball and the offense ran out onto the field.

"What's the play?" Seth asked.

"I gotta see what they're doing," Troy said, taking a swig from his bottle. "It takes a few plays at least. Maybe a couple series of plays."

Seth nodded and turned his attention to the TV, obviously interested in the game whether Troy could predict the plays or not. Troy tried to slow his breathing and just watch, seeing the whole thing, all the players at once. The formations. The defense. The motion. The shifting. Then, hardest of all, what every player did at the snap of the ball. The patterns of movement.

The room seemed to get foggy and far away. The only thing he saw was football.

After a while, he felt Seth nudging his shoulder and he came out of his trance.

"What?" he said.

"This is great, kid," Seth said, looking at his watch and setting his empty soda bottle on the coffee table, "but I got stuff to do."

Troy turned his attention back to the screen. Georgia Tech was breaking their huddle, coming to the line with two runners in the backfield and a pair of wide receivers split wide to one side.

"Toss left," Troy said, pointing at the TV.

Seth leaned forward and watched the Georgia Tech

quarterback pivot around and toss the ball to the tail-back, who was running left.

"Shoot," Seth said.

A Georgia Tech receiver left the field and another tight end came on. Vanderbilt, their opponent, ran an extra linebacker onto the field and one of the smaller, quicker cornerbacks ran off.

Troy watched as they came to the line.

"They're gonna run that tight end up the middle of the field, between the two safeties," he said. "No, the quarterback's changing the play."

The formations shifted.

"Tight end is still running up the middle," Troy said, "but it's a decoy. The wide receiver is gonna fake like he's running deep, then come back."

The Georgia Tech quarterback snapped the ball and dropped back. He pump-faked to the tight end in the middle, then threw a bullet to the wide receiver near the sideline. The receiver stopped running at the last second and came back to make the catch.

"Holy shoot," Seth said when it happened.

Five plays later, Georgia Tech stalled on their march to the end zone and kicked a field goal. Troy had been right about every play.

"Holy crow," Seth said, "you're like a football genius.

"Kid, do you know what this means?"

CHAPTER EIGHTEEN

NEITHER OF THEM HEARD his mom's car, but the screen door squeaked and she came in with a bag of groceries. Her face turned red at the sight of the Falcons' star linebacker.

"I . . . thought I was supposed to meet you," she said to Seth. "I thought maybe something came up."

"I've been hit in the head too many times," he said, running a hand through his long hair as he got up. "I knew where you meant when you said the dirt road off Route 141 where the old-timer sells peanuts, so I figured I'd meet you."

Seth took the groceries from her. She thanked him and said to just set them on the kitchen table.

Troy's mom looked at the ball in his hands and he set it down on the coffee table.

"I gave it back to him," Seth said, coming back into the living room.

"Please," his mom said, "he needs to learn you can't do things like that."

"I traded him," Seth said. "Do you know what he can do?"

Troy's mom looked at the TV, then at Troy. She puckered her lips and slowly nodded.

"He's like the weatherman," she said. "Not always right."

"He was right for me," Seth said. "He was right about T.O., and if Bryan Scott listened to him we'd have beat Philly."

"He's a sixth grader," his mom said.

"I know you just started with the team," Seth said. "But I gotta tell you, I've only got a couple years left in this game and I want a ring, a Super Bowl championship ring. You gotta have a great team, but it's more than that. You need an edge, an angle, something special.

"He could be our edge. It's not like black magic or something. Every team uses computers to analyze tendencies and formations. He's just like a supercomputer or something."

Troy's mom winced.

"A computer?" she said.

"A genius," Seth said. "Not like a genius genius. A football genius. Normal in every other way—average."

"I threw a touchdown pass the other night thirty-eight yards in the air," Troy said, proud of his throwing arm and not liking the sound of "average."

Seth looked from Troy back to his mom and said, "He doesn't even know how—he just does it, like one of those people who can look at a spilled box of tooth-picks and tell you how many there are in two seconds. They just count them. They don't even know how."

"Well," his mom said, "it's all nice."

"Tessa," Seth said, stepping toward her, "I know you don't know me that well, but if you ask people they'll tell you I'm a pretty good guy."

"I don't doubt that," she said.

"She saw when you went to that homeless shelter on TV," Troy said, nodding his head and noticing that for some reason his mom's face went redder still.

"I've got to show the coaches," Seth said. "I mean, he could help the team."

"Oh no," his mom said. "I just got my job back. He can't have anything to do with the team. He can't go near that place. Cecilia Fetters sees him and it doesn't matter how nice Mr. Langan is. She made that clear."

"Tessa," Seth said, opening his arms, "he'll be with me. I've been here for twelve years. I'm like Mr. Falcon. When the time comes, they'll probably retire my jersey. He'll be fine. Please."

"Please, Mom," Troy said, gripping the cushion underneath him.

"I need this job," she said to Seth, throwing her hands up in the air. "I just can't take a chance. I'm sorry."

"You can't take a chance!" Troy shouted, jumping up. "A chance on me!"

"I believe you're still grounded, mister," his mom said, pointing her finger in the direction of his room.

Troy clenched his hands and said, "You want me to own up? You own up. This is something I can do. Maybe it's the one thing he gave me, and you want to stop it!"

"You're twelve years old," his mom said, pressing her lips tight.

"Seth doesn't care," Troy said, pointing at the player. "He says I can do it."

He saw his mother's expression soften, her eyes tugging down at their outside corners.

"It could be an incredible thing," Seth said in a quiet voice. "I'm not trying to make trouble."

His mom put her hands on her hips. She took a deep breath and let it out through her nose.

"Okay," she said, turning to Seth and jabbing her finger in the air, "but you have to tell them I had *nothing* to do with this."

"Come on, Troy," Seth said, stepping past Troy's mom and swinging open the door, "before she changes her mind."

They almost bowled Tate over as she came up the steps with her own football in hand.

"Hi, Troy," she said stiffly, her wide eyes glued to Seth Halloway. "Do. You. Want. To. Play. Some. Football?"

"Hey," Seth said, "a girl. Cool."

Tate grinned at him and held out the ball and a Sharpie pen. Seth looked at Troy and half his mouth curled up into a smile.

"You play with a Sharpie?" Seth asked, whipping off his signature.

"She's the kicker on my team," Troy said.

Tate puffed out her chest and said, "Eighty percent on extra points. Fifty-four on field goals, with a twenty-six yarder last season."

"Twenty-six?" Seth said, letting out a low whistle and handing her back the ball. "We should sign you."

Troy winked at Tate and climbed up into the shiny H2. Tate stood with his mom on the porch and waved to him. He waved back, and off they went down the dusty red clay drive.

At the team complex, Seth waved to the guard and they pulled into the players' empty parking lot. Seth led him through the locker room. Troy drank in the smell of leather gloves and shoes and the plastic smell from shoulder pads and helmets and the nylon of practice jerseys. It was a clean, sharp smell, nothing like the sweaty smell in the gym lockers at school. Over each locker was a nameplate. Vick–7. Brooking–56. Kerney–97. Crumpler–83.

Small stools stood in front of the lockers; each locker was the size of Troy's clothes closet at home. On the locker shelves were bottles of pills, ointments, and cologne. Uniforms hung limp from hooks and hangers over piles of turf shoes. Each player must have had a dozen pairs.

Troy touched his face, trying to bring back the feeling.

"Here, look," Seth said, stopping at his own locker and taking out a three-ring binder. He opened it and pointed to a sheet of paper covered with numbers. "It's a spreadsheet. You read it like a graph. All the different formations across the top and then the different field positions down the side. You see where they intersect and it gives you the percentage of the time they pass in that situation."

"Why are some of the numbers circled?" Troy asked, pointing at one of the numbers circled in red ink.

"I circle everything over seventy-five percent and everything under twenty-five percent. That way I know I've a three-in-four chance of being right. If I think it's a pass, I play back a little. If it's a run, I move up to the line."

"What happens when it's the one time in four you're wrong?" Troy asked.

"Trouble," Seth said. "But you play the odds when they're that good."

"But you have to memorize all these situations," Troy said.

"I know," Seth said. "Look at this."

He flipped the pages of the notebook, showing Troy dozens of charts and graphs with hundreds of red circles.

"Some chart run or pass," Seth said, turning the pages. "Some are for which way they run, right or left or up the middle. Some show when they throw deep or short, when they like to run screen passes, or fake the pass and run a draw, or make it look like they're going one way and run it back the other on a reverse."

"It's a lot," Troy said.

"That's why what you can do is incredible," Seth said, snapping the book shut and replacing it in his locker. "Come on."

Troy followed Seth out into a hall, past the weight room, and up a set of stairs. He was still thinking about all those numbers, wondering how much of it Seth could really remember, when they walked into a dark office. The man behind the desk was watching a big screen on the wall, clicking the action in a football game back and forth in slow motion.

"Coach," Seth said, "you gotta see this."

When the lights went on, Troy was staring into the dark, close-set eyes of Coach Krock.

CHAPTER NINETEEN

KROCK HEAVED HIMSELF AROUND in his chair to face them, lifting the plastic leg with both hands and letting it clump down on the floor. On his head was the small white cowboy hat turned up at the sides. He tilted it back up off his forehead.

The eyes narrowed, and in that thick southern drawl, Krock said, "What in hellfire is this kid doin' here?"

Troy eased partway behind Seth Halloway's broad back and looked out from behind him at the angry-faced coach. The shelf behind the desk was lined with pictures, trophies, and footballs, all apparently belonging to Krock. Troy studied a younger-looking Krock in an Arkansas Razorbacks uniform and another wearing a Pittsburgh Steelers uniform. The coach's hair had always been long, but thicker, and dirty blond compared to the thin faded brown that now hung limp from under the brim of his hat. As far back as college, though, Krock's face was lined with hatred.

Troy looked at the plastic ankle and the lifeless sneaker peeking out from under the desk and wondered what had happened between Krock's playing days and now.

"He's okay, Coach," Seth said, drawing the small, dark eyes away from Troy.

Seth told Krock the story, starting with the Cowboys game and the post pattern Terrell Owens ran for the winning touchdown, then ending with the plays Troy had predicted watching the Georgia Tech game on TV.

"You get a concussion, Halloway?" Krock said. "'Cause you are talking hellfire hogwash."

"Coach, is it gonna hurt to see?" Seth said. "Run the tape. Let him watch. He can tell you the next play. I'm telling you, the kid's a genius."

"The kid's a pain in my britches," Krock said. "Trouble and noise."

"Coach, you know I put more study time into game tape than any player you've got," Seth said. "It takes me all week to figure out what this kid can do in two seconds, and I'm lucky if I'm right half the time whether it's a run play or a pass play. He *knows*."

"This game is about bein' physical," Krock said, glaring at Seth. "You're like every player who gets old. You want to turn it into a little schoolboy chess match, but it's a street fight. That's all this game is."

"Coach, can you imagine a street fighter who knows if his opponent is going to throw an uppercut instead of a jab?"

Krock looked sideways at Troy, scooped up his remote control, and spun back toward the screen. The lights went out, and Seth pulled the two chairs away from the front of the desk so he and Troy could sit down. Krock started running the film.

"He needs a few plays to get the rhythm," Seth said.

"Now he needs a few plays," Krock said, snorting. "Sure he does."

Troy's palms began to sweat. He tried to focus on the film, the plays being run. He tried to see it all.

"Well?" Krock said after three plays.

"Coach, let him watch," Seth said. "He sees what's coming from the patterns. It's like ESP."

"Christmas," Krock said under his breath, shaking his head.

Troy said nothing; he took deep breaths and let them out slow. He focused his eyes on the figures moving across the screen. He saw the patterns of each play as it happened, but together, as a series, they didn't mesh.

"That's six," Krock said in a bored tone. "They're getting ready to score. What's he think they're gonna do? I think *I* know. Want me to tell you? Come on. Game's on the line."

Krock started snapping his fingers, his hand held out in front of Troy's face.

"Troy?" Seth said, putting a hand on Troy's shoulder. "What do you think?"

Troy felt his eyes welling up. His brain grew hot. He opened his mouth. Nothing came out.

He shook his head.

"Bootleg play coming, I guess," Krock said with one final snap, looking back at the screen.

Seth nudged him, but Troy didn't see it. The pattern just wasn't there.

Krock ran two more plays and the offense scored on a bootleg. Troy felt his ears burning up.

"There!" Krock cried. "Got it. You don't need the kid—you got a coach with ESP, Halloway."

Seth stood, looking down at Troy in the glow of the screen. "You sure?"

Troy couldn't look at the linebacker. He could only shake his head and look down at his feet.

Krock chuckled to himself, still clicking the film back and forth. "Go on, Seth. That kid pulled the wool on you. Give him an autograph and say good-bye. Kid is like a bad penny."

Seth angled his head toward the door and Troy

followed him out. They went down the same stairs and marched through the locker room.

"Can I use the bathroom?" Troy asked.

Seth pulled up, rolled his eyes, and pointed toward a tiled opening in the middle of the locker room. When Troy came out, Seth was tapping his foot and looking at his watch. He gave Troy a curt nod and they left the building.

As they rumbled down the dirt drive off Route 141, Seth blew a small stream of air through his puckered lips.

"I'm sorry, kid," he said. "It's not your fault. I was being stupid."

"You're not stupid," Troy said.

Seth glanced at him before turning his eyes back to the curve.

"It's a game of pressure," Seth said. "Having fun, goofing around in your living room, it's a good trick. You could probably do a little stunt for the local news or something."

"It's not a stunt," Troy said.

"If you can't do it under pressure, I'm sorry, it's a stunt," Seth said. "It's like playing. People are always making fun of kickers, but you try putting it through the goalposts with seventy thousand people screaming at you and the game on the line."

"It wasn't pressure," Troy said.

"Yeah?" Seth said. "You should have seen your face, with him snapping at you."

"It didn't make sense," Troy said.

"Well, things usually don't."

Seth pulled up in front of Troy's house. Troy saw things about it he hadn't noticed before. The tear in the screen door. The blistered, peeling paint on the trim. The spare tire his mom kept under the porch. His home was a dump. The guard shack in Seth's neighborhood was bigger.

Troy opened the truck door and asked Seth to wait just a minute. He ran into the house, past his questioning mom, and into his room for the football. When he set it on the passenger seat of the H2, Seth leaned over, tossed it back out, and told him to keep it.

As the yellow H2 drove off in a cloud of dust, Troy let out a crazy scream.

"Take your stupid ball!"

He heaved the football at the truck, but it bounced back off the tire and he was sure that Seth Halloway never even knew.

CHAPTER TWENTY

"**YOU KNOW WHAT HAPPENED** to his leg?" Nathan asked, looking at Troy and Tate with raised eyebrows.

The three of them were sitting on the rail, chucking stones at a line of bottles they'd set up in the weeds below. It was early Sunday morning, and even though it was late September, it felt like the middle of August. The sun had only just risen up over the tops of the pines, and the air was already hazy and hot. The tar smell of railroad ties filled their noses.

"Car accident?" Tate said, throwing and missing.

Nathan shook his head and said, "C'mon, you didn't hear about it? My dad said it made national news."

"Your dad's like fifty years old," Troy said, shattering one of the bottles. "We probably weren't even born."

"Well," Nathan said, taking a throw of his own and

missing, "the Steelers were playing in the NFC championship game. Krock was their middle linebacker."

"Did middle linebackers call the defensive plays back then too?" Tate asked. "Was Krock smart, like Seth Halloway?"

"Halloway's not so smart," Troy said, shattering another bottle. "If he was smart, he'd have stuck up for me and I'd be telling him the plays Baltimore's gonna run at him today."

Tate glanced at him and said, "I just meant because he calls the plays."

"They were playing the Chiefs," Nathan said, "and everyone knew the Steelers needed Krock if they were going to have a chance to win, because the Chiefs' offense had Len Dawson."

"Who?" Tate asked.

"Did they even have face masks on their helmets back then?" Troy said.

Nathan ignored him, broke a bottle of his own, and pumped his fist. "So Krock broke his leg in the last game of the regular season. The doctors told him there was no way he could play on it. Something about the break right next to a nerve or something. But Krock played. They shot him with Novocain and he goes out there and the Steelers win the game and go to the Super Bowl."

Nathan pressed his lips together and shook his head. "That was it for him. He didn't even get to play in the Super Bowl. He had a bunch of operations, but finally, whop, they had to cut it off. Right at the knee."

"Gross," Tate said.

"He looked like he was mean before he lost the leg in the pictures I saw," Troy said.

"Oh, he was," Nathan said, throwing a stone. "My dad said the other players were afraid of him, he was so mean."

"NFL players aren't *afraid*," Tate said.

"What would you know?" Nathan said.

Tate stuck out her tongue.

"See?" Nathan said. "There you go."

"She knows as much as you or me," Troy said.

Nathan rolled his eyes and whipped another stone. It landed in the weeds. "She's a kicker."

"You think it's easy to kick when you've got seventy thousand people screaming at you and the game's on the line?" Troy asked.

"I would have frozen in front of that maniac too," Tate said.

"I didn't *freeze*," Troy said.

"But you didn't know the plays," Nathan said.

"I didn't freeze," Troy said, shattering another bottle. "I just got stuck. Why did he have to do that junk anyway? Snapping his fingers in my face? I could be helping them win; then I wouldn't have to listen to that moron Jamie."

"Man, is *he* annoying," Nathan said, "with that stupid 'Falcons suck' song he sings."

"And that stupid dance," Tate said, holding her hands up in the air and flopping them around while she tilted her head and let her tongue hang out.

She stopped and threw a stone that clanked off one of the bottles, and Nathan laughed.

"At least I hit it," she said, glowering. "I gotta go anyway."

"Don't be mad," Troy said.

"I'm not. I got church," Tate said.

"I gotta go too," Nathan said. "My cousins are coming for dinner."

"Come on," Troy said. "There's only two left."

"You can break them," Nathan said, scrambling to his feet and hustling after Tate. "See you tomorrow."

Troy sat and watched them walk away down the tracks, then he picked up a handful of rocks and walked right over to the bottles, blasting them at close range.

When he walked up through the pines his mom's car was already gone, and he saw his grandfather's small blue pickup truck in its place. Troy jumped onto the porch and threw open the screen door. Gramps was in the kitchen. His grandfather was strong and wiry, with the leathery arms and neck of a farmer, even though he was an auto mechanic. His hair was mostly gone, but there was a fire in his blue eyes that made him seem much younger than his seventy years. Troy ran into his arms and let the iron grip squeeze the air right out of his chest.

"There's my quarterback," his grandfather said, holding him out at arm's length and looking him over. "Give me the grip."

Troy clasped hands with him and bore down with every ounce of strength he had. His grandfather's hand was a vise, and after half a minute, Troy cried out and they laughed together.

"Did you see my scarecrow?" his grandfather asked.

"Already?"

His grandfather shrugged and walked through the screen door, pulling the stuffed figure from the bed of his truck. Its corn-husk stuffing rustled as he propped it up into one of the crooked lawn chairs on the porch.

"Halloween's not for a while, Gramp," Troy said.

"About a month too early, I know, but they took the corn in early." Gramp adjusted the scarecrow and stood back to take a look. "It'll last. Come on. You hungry?"

Troy laughed and followed his grandfather back inside.

"Your mother left *me* in charge of lunch," his grandfather said, eyeing the refrigerator suspiciously.

"We can heat up spaghetti," Troy said.

"Then watch the game," his grandfather said, rubbing his hands together and bending down to look into the fridge. His gramp was as big a Falcons fan as there was.

"Wanna go fishing?" Troy asked.

His grandfather turned to him slowly and said, "This is me. Did I ever tell you about the time my mother caught me painting our neighbor's dog with orange paint? Boys do things. That's no reason to stop living, or being a Falcons fan, which in my mind is one and the same."

Troy rolled his eyes. "It's not what I did. I'm just tired of football. Practice, practice, practice. It doesn't matter how good you are, it doesn't matter how much you know. You don't get to play quarterback around here unless you got a dad to be the coach."

His grandfather turned back to the fridge. He removed a big yellow bowl and emptied the tangle of spaghetti and red sauce into a saucepan on the stove. He turned on the flame and began stirring.

"Mike Vick's dad didn't coach his team," his grandfather said, glancing over at him. "It worked out okay for him."

"Mom brings home a hundred sports pages every night, Gramp," Troy said. "I'm sick of it. Falcons this. Falcons that. They couldn't win a game if it fell in their laps."

His grandfather set the spoon down. He took two Cokes out of the fridge, popped off the caps, and sat down at the kitchen table, pushing one of them toward Troy.

"Have a drink," he said. "And tell me what happened."

Troy sat down and sighed.

"Gramp, who's my dad?"

His grandfather filled his mouth with soda, swishing it gently around and looking out the window above the sink before he swallowed and said, "Not a bad guy. Just didn't want the same things as your mother is all."

"You mean, he didn't want me?"

His grandfather looked right at him, his pupils tight little holes in the pale-blue eyes magnified just a bit by his glasses.

"Wild horses couldn't keep your mom from you," he said. "That's a lot more'n most people ever have."

He studied Troy's face, then added, "It's different for men."

"You're a man," Troy said.

He nodded. "And I'd walk through a lake of fire for you. Everyone has things they don't have, things they want. I'm not saying it's easy, but try to look at what you have, me—your mom."

Troy bit his lip and sipped his soda, setting it back down on the water ring it had made on the table.

"I thought I was, like, a football genius," he said, sighing. "Maybe the one good thing he gave me. The only good thing."

"Your dad was a smart man," his grandfather said. "That much I know. A math major, I think."

"A football player?"

"Can't say for sure. I really didn't know him, Troy."

"Well," Troy said, shrugging and picking up his soda again, "it doesn't matter anyway. Whatever I thought I had I don't."

"Meaning?"

Troy told him about Seth Halloway, about the Falcons-Cowboys game, about the Georgia Tech game on TV, and about Coach Krock.

"Everyone gets nervous."

"I wasn't just nervous, Gramp," Troy said, squeezing the cola bottle tight. "I didn't see it."

His grandfather just stared and raised his eyebrows before he took a sip of his drink and wiped his mouth on the back of his sleeve.

"What was the game you were watching with the coach?"

"I don't know," Troy said.

"Maybe it wasn't a game," his grandfather said.

"It was."

"A real game?"

"What do you mean, Gramp?"

"What kind of game doesn't have a pattern?"

"Gramp, I hate riddles."

"What about a preseason game?" his grandfather said, a small smile on his face until he took a swig of the cola. "No rhyme or reason to preseason games. They just run a list of plays that has nothing to do with a strategy to win. It's like a practice, right?"

Troy stood up. He was breathing fast.

"Gramp," he said, "the Falcons game."

"Just started," his grandfather said, heading for the living room. "Let's see if you're not a genius after all."

As they watched, Troy predicted the other team's plays and told his gramps what the Falcons should be doing about it. If someone on the team had been there to listen, the Falcons could have won. As it was, they lost by two touchdowns. And when the TV cameras showed a close-up of Seth Halloway's miserable expression at the end of the game, Troy said it served him right.

CHAPTER TWENTY-ONE

"SWEETHEART," GRAMP SAID TO Troy's mom, "I know you don't like me to tell you what to do, but you've got to make them listen."

"You're not serious," his mother said, looking from Troy to Gramp.

"Tell her, Gramp," Troy said.

They were sitting around the kitchen table, a box of ribs from Fat Matt's Rib Shack between them. Troy's mom had picked them up on her way back from the Dome after the Falcons' loss. Troy had waited until their meal was almost finished. He knew his mom was easier to deal with when she wasn't hungry.

"Tessa," Gramp said, "if they had him there today, they would have won."

"Dad, we've been through this," she said, tossing a

bone onto her plate. "If it doesn't work all the time, it doesn't do anyone any good. It's a fun diversion, but that's all."

Gramp explained his theory about preseason games and the tape Troy must have watched with Coach Krock.

"He's special, Tessa."

"I know he's special, Dad."

"Not just special. A genius."

"Stop it!" his mother yelled, slamming her palm on the table and rattling the silverware.

The crickets chirped outside in the dusk. Troy licked his fingers and got up from the table. He took his plate to the sink, scraped it off, and loaded it into the dishwasher. His mom had settled in her place, glaring at Gramp. Troy slipped outside with the old football he used for throwing at the tire. He started up close, zipping the ball, hitting the edge of the tire, and retrieving it from the pine needles before trying again.

It took him seven times to fire one through. He took a step back, marked the spot by digging his heel into the dirt, and started again. Part of him listened to the rise and fall of their voices from the kitchen. He'd moved back seven more paces by the time Gramp swung open the screen door and marched out to his truck. Troy watched for his mom in the doorway, but she never appeared. Gramp started the truck and rolled down the window, signaling for Troy to come close.

"When she was your age," Gramp said, narrowing

his eyes at the house, "she took a bus all the way to Birmingham after we said she couldn't go. They had a Martin Luther King Day celebration there. We thought she was too young, but she did it anyway.

"You should've seen your gram," he said, shaking his head. "Her head about exploded, but when it came time to punish her, you know what I realized? I realized she was right about that celebration. It was important for people to show their support, and she was old enough to go."

"What's that got to do with this?" Troy asked.

Gramp looked at him hard. "Sometimes grown-ups' vision gets cloudy from the smog of the world. Sometimes a kid's heart tells him to do something and he needs to listen, even if it means getting in trouble."

"What am I supposed to do?" Troy asked.

"I don't know, exactly," Gramp said. "But you'll know when you think of it. You'll just know. Now, I gotta get out of here before she throws a rock through my windshield. I'm kidding. It'll be dark soon, and I don't like driving in the dark no more."

Troy hugged his grandfather's neck and kissed his bristly cheek, then watched the small pickup disappear. When he turned back to the tire, Tate was standing there.

"Don't sneak up on me," he said.

She shrugged and picked up the ball, throwing a wobbly pass at the tire, missing completely.

"Now you go get it," Troy said to her.

"Don't get hot. I'll shag them for you," Tate said, scrambling into the trees for the ball and chucking it out to him.

Troy fired. Right through. He took a step back and marked it with his heel.

"What's going on?" Tate asked.

Troy told her everything.

"If they hadn't blocked that hole," he said, bouncing a pass off the tire's rim, "I'd go try to talk to Seth."

"Call him," Tate said.

"It's too easy to say no on the phone," Troy said. "I need to talk to him in person."

"Would he listen?"

"I'd make him listen," Troy said. "But it doesn't matter. I'm locked out."

"If somebody plugged that hole," Tate said, "why can't we just *un*plug it? You've got tools in that shed."

"Even with them, it'd take all night. My mom would call the police and kill me."

"All night for what?" Nathan said, stepping out from around the side of the house closest to the path in the woods.

"Not for three of us," Tate said, grinning.

At first, they picked at the new concrete with the chisels from Troy's shed. They spoke carefully in whispers and set the pieces down gently in the weeds. But by the time they could see through to the other side, Nathan was swinging away with a sledgehammer

116

and Troy and Tate were tossing the rubble into a pile. The pocking sound of the hammer echoed down the length of the moonlit concrete wall.

"Can you get through yet?" Nathan said, wiping his sweaty brow and peering through the hole.

"I'm not that skinny," Troy said.

"Well, I gotta be home before nine," Nathan said, looking at the glowing piece of moon.

"Work, don't talk," Tate said.

Ten minutes later, Nathan held his wristwatch out at them and said, "I *gotta* go. For real."

Tate put her hands on her hips and said to Troy, "Can you get through that?"

Troy put his hands on the broken edges and started to squeeze through. Wiggling his shoulders, he just made it. He wormed the rest of his body through, hanging down with his hands in the grass until he could free his feet.

He fell with a thud.

From the other side, Tate called, "You okay?"

"I'm fine," Troy said, brushing off and whispering back through the crack. "I'll see you tomorrow, in school."

Then he turned and headed into the night.

CHAPTER TWENTY-TWO

CRICKETS AND CICADAS BUZZED in Troy's ears. He pushed aside the needles of a pine tree on the edge of Seth Halloway's lawn and stopped to catch his breath. There were lights on in the two lower levels of the house.

A stick snapped behind him. Troy spun, his heart leaping, panic lifting him off the ground as he backed away.

"Hssss."

He scrambled backward toward Seth Halloway's lawn and fell over a bush. Without getting up, he crabbed backward toward the pool. The image of a horrible snake—worse, some crazy monster from a nightmare—forced a low moan up out of his throat.

"Hssss!"

He groaned.

"Troy," came an urgent whisper.

Troy froze. "Tate? Are you crazy?"

The pine branches parted and there she stood.

"You scared the heck out of me," Troy said, getting up from the ground. "What happened?"

"We figured you better have someone to watch your back, and Nathan's butt's too big to get through," she said, grinning. "So here I am."

Troy ran his hand over his face, shaking his head. "Well, come on, then."

"What are you going to do?"

"Ring the bell, I guess," Troy said.

They crept around the outside of the house. On the ground level by the pool was a big room with sliding glass doors. Inside was Seth Halloway with three other players, sitting around on an L-shaped sectional couch, watching the *Sunday Night Football* game with three teammates. Each of them had one or more bags of ice packed onto his body. Seth had four. Two on his knees, one on the elbow, and the last he held against his ribs.

Tate gripped his arm and said, "That's Patrick Kerney, John Abraham, and Demarrio Williams."

Troy looked at her in the glow of the light, then back at the big men to study their faces.

"How can you tell without their numbers?" he asked.

She shrugged. "You think I just trade those cards? I study them."

Troy motioned with his hand for her to follow. They rounded the house, checking the street for a sign of anyone who might stop them or call security. The street was empty and dark. Troy climbed the stone steps and stood in front of the door, breathing hard. He tried to slow down his breathing, but finally just rang the bell.

The bell chimed deep inside the house. No one came. Troy tried again. *Ding dong.*

After another minute, Tate stepped up and jabbed the bell over and over until they heard noises from inside.

"Tate," Troy said, pulling her hand away. "Are you kidding?"

The door swung open. Seth Halloway said, "Kid, are you crazy?"

"Yes," Troy said, staring at him hard. "Crazy and a genius, at least at football."

Seth rolled his eyes and shook his head. "We been through this, buddy. Where's your mom, anyway? She's not going to be happy, you know."

"I know," Troy said. "But no one will be happy if you guys keep losing. I can help. It was a preseason game, that's why I couldn't call it. With Krock."

"Kid," Seth said, sighing long and loud. "This is like my weekend. Film and meetings tomorrow, and

Tuesday's my only day off. It's like Friday night to me. I'm not happy we lost. My ribs are killing me. My elbow. Both knees. I'm gonna go back inside now and pretend you didn't bust in here again, because I like you and I like your mom, but you better get on home and let me enjoy what time I do have. And take your girlfriend too."

Seth started to turn and close the door, but Tate jammed her foot against it and it bounced back open. She stepped up onto the threshold and kicked Seth Halloway in the leg.

He cried out in pain.

"You big dummy," she said. "You do those United Way commercials talking about how important it is to help kids. So why can't you help now? Or is that just some phony line for TV?"

Seth was hopping on one foot, grabbing his knee and groaning. When he got his footing, he whipped out his cell phone and started to dial.

"You gonna call the cops?" Tate asked, scowling.

"You bet," Seth said.

"Good," she said, crossing her arms and planting her feet. "I can't wait to tell the reporters when they ask me what happened. How you don't really care about kids."

Seth's brow wrinkled, and he looked from Tate to Troy. "Is she for real?"

"Pretty much," Troy said with a quick nod of his head.

"Well . . . well," Seth said, snapping his phone shut. "Shoot. Two crazy kids. One crazier than the other. What do you want from me? Won't you just leave?"

"I want you to give my friend a chance," Tate said, glaring up at him. "He told you what happened. Don't you listen?"

"Preseason, whatever," Seth said, pocketing the phone, "the pressure made him crack. Look, I'd love nothing more than for you to be this football genius thing, kid. But the game's about pressure."

"He can do it," Tate said.

Troy nodded his head.

"Yeah," Seth said. "Okay, here's the deal. You come in and you call the plays. I got three other players inside watching the game. That's pressure. Then, if you mess up, I call security and they take you out of here and call your mom and I never see you again."

"That's mean," Tate said, stomping her foot.

"No," Seth said. "That's pressure. I got a life, you know. I can't have you two showing up every time he thinks he gets it right. You gotta decide. That's it."

"Okay," Tate said, grabbing Troy by the arm and tugging him inside. "He'll do it."

CHAPTER TWENTY-THREE

"TATE," TROY SAID, FROWNING at her.

"You will," she said. "Come on. I know you will."

"He better," Seth said, hobbling back into the house, grabbing at his knee. "And I better be able to lift weights tomorrow."

He led them down some curved stairs to the ground floor and the big media room. The players didn't pay any attention to them; their eyes were glued to the game. The coffee table was covered with empty bottles. Two big bowls were half full, one with chips, one with pretzels, and a round container of dip sat between them with streaks of the stuff spattered around it.

Demarrio Williams looked up and said, "Hey, kid."

The others noticed them and did the same but went right back to the TV.

"Aren't you going to ask us to sit down?" Tate said, still glaring at Seth. "Maybe if we want a drink or something? My mom would kill me if I had your manners."

Seth twisted up his mouth and somewhat sarcastically waved his hand toward the couch and said, "Won't you please sit down, Madam Queen?"

"Thank you," Tate said primly. She patted the cushion next to her, looking back at Troy and motioning with her head.

"And to drink, Your Majesty?" Seth said, bowing.

The players all looked sideways at him, chuckling, then right back to the game.

"Iced tea is fine," Tate said. "Arizona Green Tea, if you have that."

Seth made a circle with his mouth and put his hand to it, gasping and raising his eyebrows. "Can Her Majesty forgive me? Nestea is all I have."

Tate shrugged and nodded, turning her attention to the TV. The Jets were playing the Giants.

"Okay for you too?" Seth asked Troy, going behind the bar and opening the refrigerator there.

Troy nodded and sat beside Tate. He nudged her ribs with his elbow and said, "Take it easy, will you?"

"Just do your genius thing," she said, "and don't worry about me. When you're a girl, you gotta assert yourself. That's what my mom says. Watch."

Seth set the drinks down in front of them.

"Yes, I would like some chips, thank you," Tate said, looking up at him.

Seth crossed his arms, staring back at her. Finally, he laughed and grabbed the bowl, setting it in front of them.

"Just in case," he said, pushing the dip her way too.

Then Seth stepped back and took out his cell phone again.

"Hello? Harvey?" he said into the phone. "Yes, this is Seth Halloway at 2112 Jackson Drive. I may have a problem, Harvey, and I just wanted to see if you might be able to send a man over here."

Seth looked at them, raising an eyebrow, and said, "No, not right yet. I'll call you. The problem might take care of itself. I'll see. Just wanted to check. Thanks."

Seth snapped the phone shut again. He put his hands on his knees and leaned close, staring at Troy. "Pressure."

Troy clenched his teeth and turned his attention to the game. The Giants runner Tikki Barber ran the ball across the fifty to the forty-five, giving his team a first down. Troy watched the defense change players.

He let the room drift away and his mind soak up what he saw without thinking. The Giants came out with two running backs, two tight ends, and only one wide receiver.

"Angle route weak to Tikki," he said, describing the pass pattern that would look like a sideways V if drawn on the chalkboard, "with Toomer on a deep crossing pattern as the secondary route."

He didn't really see, but felt the Falcons players' eyes go from him back to the TV. The Giants ran the angle route, with Manning completing the pass to Tikki. Tate jumped up and whooped. Troy focused on the game.

The Giants didn't change players. The Jets brought in an extra linebacker and took a cornerback out.

"Jets will blitz Manning from the weak side with that linebacker who just came in," Troy said, his voice sounding distant, coming out in a flat tone from his trance. "He'll either get sacked or pass it to the tight end down the seam."

It happened the way he said it would, Manning getting mowed down by the blitzing backer before he could get off the pass.

"Did you see the tight end run free up the middle? Right up the seam?" Demarrio Williams said to Seth. "Just like the kid said."

"I did," Seth said, crossing his arms, looking from the TV, to Troy, and back, "and the sack. What now?"

Troy didn't even have to see what players the Giants were going to use.

"That same screen pass, but this time to the fullback going the other way, to the weak side," Troy said.

He was right.

The Falcons players let out a cheer, and Tate slapped him on his back. Seth tossed the cell phone over his shoulder. As it clattered on the floor, he asked if the kids wanted some leftover pizza.

CHAPTER TWENTY-FOUR

SETH DROPPED TATE OFF in front of her apartment building, but not before he held out his hand and she
slapped him five.

"I was just saying that stuff," she said, grinning.
"You're everybody's hero. You still would be, no matter
what some girl kicker says."

"Well, I'd hate to think how mean you'd be if you
were an offensive lineman," he said. "But the best
thing about sports is the friends you make, so I figure
Troy here is pretty lucky."

"Her too," Troy said, and they all had a laugh.

Troy liked riding up high in the H2. He wished
Jamie Renfro could see him, sitting there with Seth
Halloway. Troy looked over at the player's face, the
muscled jaw.

"So, you got a girlfriend?" Troy said without thinking.

Seth's face colored just a bit. He glanced at himself in the rearview mirror, then looked at Troy.

"A couple girls you might call friends, I guess. Nothing serious."

"You got kids?" Troy asked.

"Hey, not me," Seth said.

"If you did, you probably wouldn't just take off like they were never born, I bet."

They rode for a few minutes in silence before Seth said, "No. Probably not. But sometimes things happen that people can't help."

"Like what?" Troy asked. "Like aliens come down in a spaceship and take you away?"

Seth shrugged. "I'm no school psychologist, kid. All I know is, things happen. Unless you're the one they're happening to, you usually can't understand it. Most people are good people. I believe that, and now we're at your driveway."

They pulled off Route 141 and started down the twisty dirt lane.

"You wanna just let me out here?" Troy asked.

"Why's that?"

"Just better if I get out and walk from here," Troy said. "I'd rather tell my mom about all this when the time's right."

"Which is when?" Seth asked, slowing down.

"I don't know," Troy said. "Not now."

"You gonna lie?" Seth asked, stopping the truck.

"No. I'm just not gonna say anything," Troy said.

"What if she asks?"

"Then I'll think of something," Troy said.

Seth stared at him for a minute, then asked, "Want me to do you a favor?"

"What favor?" Troy asked.

"It's something good," Seth said. "Trust me."

"Sure."

"Okay," Seth said. He put the truck into drive and started toward the house.

"Hey," Troy said, bracing his hands on the dash. "She'll ground me for life."

"You want to do something," Seth said, glancing at him, "you gotta do it right. You don't start right, you won't finish right."

"What's the favor you're doing for *me*?"

"This is the favor," Seth said. "Making you tell the truth. It's something pretty important that you need to know."

"I know that already," Troy said, slumping down into the seat and turning his head toward the door. "You don't think I know?"

"You know," Seth said, "but what you don't know is that it's important enough to get in trouble over. The truth is more important than the trouble it brings. The truth is everything.

"If you and I are gonna do something," Seth said,

"we gotta do it right. Just tell her the truth. I got your back."

They pulled up in front of the house. The door swung open and his mom stepped out onto the porch, hands on her hips.

"Troy? What in the world?"

"It's okay," Seth said, holding up his hands to calm her.

"You told me you and your friends were walking the tracks," she said, glaring at Troy.

"We were!" Troy insisted. "And then . . . then . . ."

The answer came to him, slick and easy. A story about Tate going through the wall earlier in the day to see Seth's house and later realizing she lost the necklace her mom let her wear and her being in tears and begging Troy to go back with her to help find it and him feeling sorry for her and how he knew it was right to stick by your friends when they were in trouble.

"Then what?" his mother asked.

Troy swallowed. "The truth is, I wanted to go to Seth's to show him what I showed Gramp."

He looked up at Seth, who grinned and nodded his head.

"Tessa," Seth said, talking fast, "he is what he says. It was a preseason game Krock showed him. I thought it was pressure. You should have seen him just now. The guys are over, watching *Sunday Night Football*. He nailed it! He's a genius. A football genius. I'm not kidding."

His mom studied Seth for a minute before finally saying, "Do you want to come in?"

"I want to talk to you," Seth said, following her through the door.

"Coke?" she asked, leading them into the kitchen and pulling out a chair for Seth.

"Sure," Seth said, sitting down.

His mom opened two bottles and set them down on the table. She poured a glass of milk for Troy and put out a plate of her special chocolate chips made with dark chocolate. Then she sat down, put her elbows on the table, and braced her chin on her hands.

"He's twelve," she said, as if that were the beginning and the end of an argument. "I need this job."

"We had a rough start with Krock," Seth said. "But he's not the head coach. That's my plan. Go right to Coach McFadden."

"Didn't they bring Krock in because if Coach McFadden doesn't win, he's going to replace him? Even I know that," Troy's mom said. "Playing one off against the other? There's almost no way you can win and lots of ways you can lose."

"When they see what he can do, we'll all win," Seth said. He pushed the Coke aside and leaned toward Troy's mom with his muscular arms on the table. "We're oh and two, but we're a good team. With Mike Vick, and Troy, we could win it all. Everything. You know what that means?"

"I'd like the team to win," his mom said, "don't get me wrong. But winning or losing doesn't make or break me. Losing this job does. If this falls through, my old job is already gone. I've got bills. A mortgage. Credit cards."

"Mom," Troy said.

"Okay, okay," Seth said, holding up his hands. "I'll put my money where my mouth is. Ten grand. I get that as a bonus for every quarterback sack, so it's not that big a deal. If this doesn't work and you lose your job, that'll give you enough to get things going."

Troy looked at the player's face. Seth wore an easy smile and the eyes of a man who was used to helping people out of jams, happy to do it. Then he looked at his mom and watched the storm roll in. Her mouth turned down and her eyes got squinty.

"You can take that Coke with you, thank you very much," she said in a slow, seething voice. Her arm extended slowly out and her finger unfurled, pointing toward the door. "I won't tell you what you can do with it."

"What'd I say?" Seth said, touching his fingers to his chest.

"I've gone twelve years without handouts from *any* man," she said. "I sure as heck am not going to start now. You think I was asking you for money? Please. Just leave."

"I didn't mean—"

"I'm doing just fine. I didn't ask you to come here, remember? I know you're a big NFL star and people don't ask you to leave, but I'm asking and I'd appreciate it if you'd go. Now."

Seth clamped his mouth shut.

"Mom," Troy said when he could finally speak.

"You?" she said, shooting her eyes at him. "Lying. Sneaking around. Is this how I raised you? Gift from your father? Maybe that's it. Not listening. The gift of putting yourself before everyone else."

Seth's chair scraped back and he stood up. Troy's mom looked down at the table, still pointing her finger toward the door. Seth walked out, letting the screen door slam behind him, and a fat tear spattered the place mat beneath his mom's nose.

Troy felt too wounded by her words to feel sorry for her tears.

CHAPTER TWENTY-FIVE

IF HAVING SETH WALK out on him wasn't unpleasant enough, Troy got to look forward to giving Jamie the ball he owed him the next day at school. He'd rather give up the ball, though, than listen to Jamie and his friends calling him a welcher all day long. When he did hand it over, Jamie sniffed and turned it over in his hands before jamming it into his locker and slamming it shut.

"Too bad they suck so much or I could sell it for a couple bucks," Jamie said with a mean smile as he spun the combination dial on his locker. "Nobody really cares about a team that hasn't won a game and probably won't all season. A ball like that from the Cowboys would go for at least five hundred. For this thing, I'd be lucky to get five."

"Too bad none of the Cowboys would know you or your dad if you fell on them," Troy said. "Then you wouldn't have to worry about paying money to get a ball from your favorite team."

"Like you know these guys," Jamie said, turning toward him with a sneer.

"Seth Halloway was at my house," Troy said.

"Whatever," Jamie said, and walked away.

Troy wanted to throw a book at the back of his head, but didn't. He knew that wasn't the way to really fix Jamie, and he knew he wasn't going to get the chance to outshine him on the football field. What would stuff a cork in his hole would be for the Falcons to win and for Troy to be there, helping them do it. He thought of a way he could pull it off, even without his mom's help. It would be daring, but as Troy thought about it through the rest of the school day, he figured he had nothing to lose.

On the bus ride home from school, Troy shared the plan with his friends. Tate didn't like it. She had to go home to watch her little sister anyway, but she thought he was only digging himself in deeper. Troy said he was already in the basement and was able to convince Nathan to come over and help him.

"All you have to do is sit here and play Madden 2006 with the volume up," Troy said when they reached his room. "Is that so hard?"

"What if she comes in?"

"We'll lock the door," Troy said. "I'm the one taking the chance. Your dad's not going to send *you* to military school."

"He'll take my bike," Nathan said, sitting down and crossing his legs. "He did it before."

"You ate your sister's guppies," Troy said.

"*You* dared me."

"Okay, so I dare you to stay here in my room and pretend you're me. Happy? I need this," Troy said, handing him the controller. "Come on."

Nathan took it and started to play.

"I don't know," he said, but his eyes were already fixed to the screen. The game was running.

"Good," Troy said, locking the bedroom door and backing up toward his window. "Just like that. Don't say a word if she calls. She'll leave you alone. As long as she can hear you playing the game, you're fine. She'll think you're me giving her the silent treatment."

Nathan shrugged without looking up. He leaned with the player he controlled on the screen and barked out "Yes" as he scored a touchdown. Troy opened the latch and forced the window open, slipping out and dropping to the ground. He dusted off his hands and started down the path for Cotton Wood Country Club. It took him only ten minutes to get to Seth's place, and two of those minutes were spent wiggling through the hole in the wall. The rest was on a dead run.

He rang the bell and Seth came to the door, wearing

Falcons shorts and no shirt, crunching an apple. On the front and back of both his knees were ice bags wrapped in place with Ace bandages.

"Hey," he said, swinging open the door and saluting him with the apple in hand. "Private Troy, reporting for duty, huh? Why am I not surprised? My day off and here you are. Unannounced."

"You said Coach McFadden could help us," Troy said, trying to catch his breath. "Let me show him."

His hands were on his knees and he was bent over in an effort to catch his breath.

"And your mom will then . . . what? Ship you off and claw out my eyes?" Seth said. "No blind men yet in the NFL, kid. I pass."

"What if McFadden says it's okay? How can they blame my mom? They'll blame you, if anyone," Troy said.

"Nice," Seth said.

"You know what I mean," Troy said. "No one can do anything to you."

"You'd be amazed, kid. That's how the NFL works. N-F-L, Not For Long. Especially when you get a little long in the tooth, like me."

"Long in the what?" Troy said.

"The tooth," Seth said, "like a gopher. They get old, their teeth get long. Let me get a shirt and I'll be right down."

CHAPTER TWENTY-SIX

EXCEPT FOR THE GLOW of the big screen, Coach McFadden's office was dark. Troy's palms began to sweat. His mouth went dry.

"Coach?" Seth said, pushing the door wide open. "I gotta show you something."

McFadden was sitting at his desk but facing the side wall. He spun their way and flipped on the light. Seth gasped and pulled up short. Troy bumped right into him, then saw why Seth had stopped so suddenly. Sitting on the leather couch at the far side of the big office was Coach Krock.

"Seth," McFadden said, "what can I do for you?"

"I . . . didn't know you were busy," Seth said, looking from the head coach to Krock and back.

"Carl and I were just going over some film,"

McFadden said. He stood up and shook Seth's hand, then adjusted his glasses and looked at Troy. "Who's this?"

"A kid I met," Seth said. "You gotta see what he can do, Coach. He's like a genius. A football genius."

McFadden chuckled and said, "Well, we got the Saints coming up and any ideas on how to slow them down are welcome.

"Wherever it comes from," he added, looking over the tops of his glasses at Troy, obviously amused.

"Oh, bull crap," Krock said, leaning back in his chair and splaying his plastic leg out to the side. "I seen this parlor trick, Bart. Don't waste your time."

"It's not a trick," Seth said, glaring at Krock until McFadden cleared his throat.

"Run a couple plays, Coach," Seth said to McFadden. "Go ahead. I'm serious."

Krock snorted and shook his head, muttering something about work.

"We got work to do, Seth," McFadden said, his face turning serious.

"Please, Coach. You have to."

McFadden shrugged, nodded his head, and went back to his chair. He flipped off the light and ran the film. One play. Two. Three. Four.

Krock started to snigger.

"Sweep left," Troy said, looking at the three men quickly before turning his attention back to the screen.

It was a sweep. To the left.

"Probably saw that game on TV, Bart," Krock said. "You get that dish, you can see them all."

"Coach," Seth said, "I've seen him do it live. He did it with the Georgia Tech game on Saturday and the Giants-Jets game on *Sunday Night Football*. He can do it with any game, just not preseason."

"Why?" the head coach asked. "No strategy in a preseason game?"

"I think," Troy said.

McFadden nodded and got up from his desk. He walked over to his bookcase and removed a cassette from a high shelf.

"I know he didn't see this game, Carl," McFadden said to Krock. "He wasn't born when this was on."

McFadden put in the tape and let it run. After six offensive plays, Troy began to tell them what the next ones were going to be. He got ten plays in a row right.

"What'd you call him?" McFadden asked Seth, turning off the machine.

"A genius," Seth said, "a football genius. All the tendencies and formations that we study and plug into computers, his brain just calculates it all. Instantly. But he does it better than the computers. We just get little bits of it, like whether in a certain formation on third down they're more likely to run or pass.

"He calculates it all. Everything. What yard line they're on. The positions of the players. Formations.

And what they've run on the previous plays. You know every coach has his game plan scripted out to run certain plays in certain situations? It's like he sees a little of what they're doing and his mind fills in all the blanks. He knows the whole game plan. All he needs is to see a few plays to get the pattern."

"My mom says it's like the weather," Troy said. "I say ESP."

"Your mom?" Coach McFadden said.

"She's the new PR assistant," Seth said. "That's how I found him. He was the one on the sideline at the Cowboys game."

"I tried to tell everyone they were going to run T.O. to the outside instead of to the inside," Troy said, getting excited.

"All right," Krock said, growling and rising to his feet with a clank from the metal joints in his leg. "That's enough. We're oh and two and we haven't had a winning season in three years. Now you're going to bring a twelve-year-old in to save us?"

"You gotta take this chance, Coach," Seth said. "We could win it all with this kid."

"Carl, go ahead and sit down, okay?" McFadden said.

"My leg makes it more comfortable for me to stand, Coach," Krock said, "if you don't mind."

"Sure, sure. Just be comfortable."

"I doubt that, Bart," Krock said, glancing at Troy. "I specifically told that little brat there to stay away from me and stay away from this team. I told Halloway that the last time he brought him around. Now here they are again, talking to you. This kid *cost* us the Cowboys game, running around the sideline, distracting everyone, causing confusion. The police had to take him."

"That's a lie!" Troy said, leaning toward Krock. "I tried to tell you the play."

Krock turned his head sideways and shot a glare at Troy from his near eye. Troy remembered Nathan's words. NFL players were afraid of this guy. Now he knew why.

"I grew up on a pig farm," Krock said through his teeth. "Never knew one that didn't make a stink. I used to wait for slaughter day like it was Christmas, and I'm looking that way for the day I don't have to see this one."

"Carl—" Coach McFadden said.

"Don't do this to yourself, Bart," Krock said, holding up his hand. "I respect what you done, as a player and a coach. Don't go out this way."

"Carl, you saw what he just did," McFadden said.

"Can you imagine the newspapers?" Krock snorted. "What they'll say on TV? They'll laugh you out of coaching. You won't get a high school job by the time it was done."

"No one would have to know, Carl," McFadden said. "We could turn this season around. We could win the whole thing if he can do what I just saw him do. If that happened, you'd get the next head coach job that opened up."

"But Bart," Krock said, his sarcastic drawl sweet and slow, like pancake syrup, "I'm happy right here, bein' your assistant. Until Mr. Langan says otherwise.

"But," Krock added, turning back to Troy and pointing his finger, his voice angry and quiet, "if things keep sliding and they do make me head coach of this team? Well, I can feel a hankering coming on for a whole new PR department. Get rid of the whole mess of 'em."

A mean smile curled the corners of Krock's mouth. He turned and thumped out. Troy could hear him laughing to himself as he moved off down the hallway.

CHAPTER TWENTY-SEVEN

"**CAN'T YOU JUST FIRE** him?" Seth asked.

McFadden shook his head and said, "I'm in no position to fire anyone, Seth. I'm the one in trouble if we don't start winning."

"We could work around him," Seth said.

McFadden held up his hand. "I'm not going to go out that way, Seth. Carl was right—a story like that would ruin me, forever. Hey, this season isn't over. We win a couple games these next few weeks and we'll be back on track. You just think about that, Troy."

McFadden mussed Troy's hair and showed him to the door.

"And as long as I'm here, you don't have to worry about your mom. She's got a job with me, son."

Troy thanked him and Seth led him downstairs and past the empty weight room.

"Will they keep him?" Troy asked when they were alone.

"We gotta win," Seth said, swinging open the door to the locker room. "We got the Saints coming up and the Packers after that. Then the Bucs and the Panthers, all games we could win. Or lose. We lose those and he'll get fired. He could be gone in four or five weeks."

"And I gotta believe that's just what's gonna happen," said a nasty voice behind them.

They turned and saw that Krock had come out of the elevator. He was smiling in a mean way and he moved up close to them, standing almost toe-to-toe with Seth.

"'Cause it's gettin' awful hard for me to make the defensive adjustments I need for us to win these days," he said.

"You'd *lose* on purpose?" Seth said, disgusted and scowling at the same time. "How could you even think like that? You're on a *team*."

"Well," Krock said softly, touching Seth's chest, "not that I'd do it on purpose, exactly. It's just hard for me to adjust my defense when I got an overpaid veteran middle linebacker who's . . . well, I guess he's lost a step."

Seth clenched his hands. Even Troy knew that when a player got old and they said he lost a step it meant trouble. Whenever that player missed a tackle, or made a mistake, that's what people would say. And once a player had that name tagged on him, there was no fixing it. The end was very near.

"I got big, fat defensive tackles as fast as you," Krock said with a sneer.

"You know I get to the plays quicker than anyone just knowing where to go," Seth said, his voice low but starting to waver.

"I told you," Krock said softly, patting Seth gently on the shoulder, his mean smile widening. "This game ain't a chess match. It's a street fight. You *lost* a step.

" 'Bout four weeks left, little piggy," Krock said, turning to Troy, "before your momma's in the welfare line. Four weeks, tops."

Krock pushed past them, thumping through the locker room and disappearing out the far door with a shrill *"soo-eee"* pig call that vibrated the air.

Seth didn't move, and Troy stood there next to him, the sound of the call still ringing in his ears. Finally, Seth sighed and muttered a curse under his breath.

"You're still the top tackler," Troy said, following Seth across the locker room.

"If you owned an NFL team, I'd be all set," Seth said, pushing through the door.

"I'm sorry, Seth," Troy said as he climbed into the yellow H2.

"Not your fault," Seth said. "Win some, lose some."

They rode in silence until they came up to the

turnoff on Route 141 for Old River Road, the way to the Cotton Wood Country Club entrance.

"Look," Seth said, "I'm thinking your mom isn't going to want to see my face."

"I can walk from your house," Troy said.

Seth just nodded. They passed through the gates with the guard waving cheerfully. They drove down the curving streets, passing expensive cars and homes the size of small buildings that Troy could see through the trees. He sighed and picked at the tattered hem of the T-shirt he wore, then poked a finger through the hole in the leg of his jeans. The laces on his sneakers were gray. He turned his foot on the side and saw the treads were worn nearly flat.

"So," Seth said as they pulled into the driveway of his big stone house, "your mom must have a guy she sees, right?"

"No," Troy said. "I don't think she likes men in general. Outside my gramp."

"I kinda got that impression," Seth said.

"Why?" Troy said. "You think she's pretty?"

"Of course she is," Seth said, turning off the engine and putting his hands on the wheel. "But I'm far from her favorite person after what I said. You know, about the money."

"You were trying to be nice," Troy said.

Seth nodded and sighed.

"Women," he said.

"Yeah," Troy said.

Seth smiled at him and slapped both his knees before opening the truck door. "Well, at least I know where all my footballs have been going."

"I only took one," Troy said. "Honest."

"I don't care," Seth said, swatting the air. "You need a ball, you just come get one, Troy. I got plenty."

"You could come to one of my games sometime," Troy said. "I don't do much. Punt team, sometimes. Unless this jerk Jamie Renfro breaks his leg."

"Easy, killer," Seth said. "Maybe in about a month, if your mom cools down by then."

"You don't have to sit with her or anything," Troy said. "Just see the team."

"Well," Seth said, "you never know. Hey, you go easy on sneaking into this place. You get caught, they won't like it much."

Seth looked at his watch and said, "Hey, I gotta go, my man."

"What time is it?"

"Almost seven," Seth said.

"Jeez, seven? Oh, Nathan's gonna kill me," Troy said, and he took off running for the wall.

CHAPTER TWENTY-EIGHT

NATHAN STARED AT THE door to Troy's bedroom with the face of a victim in a horror movie. His eyes were as big as Ping-Pong balls. His forehead glistened with sweat. The man he was controlling on the TV screen made a mad dash around the game going the wrong way on the football field because Nathan wasn't paying attention.

Troy looked at the door too, and the sudden pounding made him jump. Nathan closed his eyes. His lips were moving in a silent prayer.

"Troy, you let me in there!" his mother screamed through the door. "I said enough is enough and I meant it! I *will* break down this door."

Troy helped Nathan to his feet and boosted him up to the window.

"She's like a crazy mule," Nathan mumbled, dropping to the ground outside with a grunt.

Troy pulled the door open. His mother stood there, breathing hard and glaring at him. He could see that her eyes were red and wet from crying, and he felt sick with guilt doing this to her.

"I'm sorry," he said.

"Sorry?" she said, arching her eyebrows. "Sorry?"

"I am," he said.

That deflated her. She turned and hunched her shoulders and walked down the short hallway into the kitchen, where she sat down at the table and cried.

Troy stepped slowly into the kitchen. Her arms were crossed, her head buried in them, shaking. Troy reached out and put his hand on hers. It went stiff, then she opened it and grasped his fingers.

Without picking her head up, she said, "Don't do that to me, Troy. Don't stop talking. Don't ever do that."

"Okay," he said quietly. "I won't."

She picked up her head and pulled him tight to her. He could feel her hair, wet with the tears, against his cheek. One of her hands was on the back of his head and he could feel the muscles in her jaw moving as she spoke.

"You're all I've got, honey," she said. "I'd die if I didn't have you with me."

Troy waited a minute, then said, "Like if I went to military school?"

She gripped him even tighter, then let up and said, "I wouldn't do that, honey. Even for your own good. I couldn't."

Troy sighed and said, "I know, Mom. The reason I didn't answer was because I just didn't hear you, Mom."

She held his shoulders and looked at his face.

"I couldn't not answer you if you needed me and I was really there," he said.

Her face wrinkled with curiosity.

A lie popped into his head, an easy way out. A story about headphones and loud music and being so into his book that he lost track of time.

Instead, he took a deep breath and said, "It was Nathan in there. I asked him to play the game so you wouldn't know I went out."

"Out where?"

"Mom, don't get excited, I'm trying to do the right thing. I went to Seth's. He didn't know I snuck out or anything, and he took me to see the head coach to show him what I can do and overrule Krock. But it didn't work. Krock was there, and mad, and if the team keeps losing and he gets to be the head coach . . ."

Troy couldn't look at her.

"Well," he said, "then he said he'd fire you."

When he glanced up, she was looking away, her lower lip pinched between her teeth.

"Maybe they won't fire Coach McFadden," she said softly. "That's what we gotta hope for, right?"

"You're not mad?" he asked.

"Oh, I guess I am," she said, even though she wore a small smile. "But I'm glad you told the truth, and I'm really glad you weren't just ignoring me. It's kind of a soft spot with me."

"Because my dad did that to you?" Troy asked before he could stop the words from leaving his mouth.

His mom's eyes shifted around and she sniffed like she didn't care all that much.

"Maybe in a way," she said, brushing something off her sleeve. "Are you hungry?"

"Sure," he said.

He set the table while she stirred a pot of chili on the stove. There was corn bread in the oven. They ate and talked about the small things that happened to them during the day, cleaned up, and played a cutthroat game of Monopoly until it was time for bed.

She didn't seem worried about losing her job. It was like she knew something, and maybe she did. Maybe Mr. Langan wouldn't fire Coach McFadden and she knew that.

As he lay there in the dark, though, the warmth of the evening with his mom began to fade. Happy thoughts were sacked by doubts. And, when he heard the lonely sound of the Midnight Express, he wondered if he'd ever get a chance to do something special, to be someone special. Or were the Coach Renfros and Coach Krocks of the world always going to be there to put him down, while men like his father and Seth Halloway walked away?

Troy didn't want to give up, but lying there by himself, it seemed like he had no choice. It wasn't until the next day, at football practice, that Tate came up with an idea.

CHAPTER TWENTY-NINE

THE SUN HAD ALREADY dropped below the trees and it was mercifully cool out. The smell of cut grass was in the air, and somewhere in the neighborhood next to the field, a lawn mower droned on. Whistles sounded from the field next to them, a high school girls soccer game in full swing.

Coach Renfro's voice cut through it all. It had been a brutal practice with lots of running and lots of hitting. Now it was time for Bull in the Ring. The whole team would circle up around one player. Coach Renfro would call out a name, and whoever it was had to run as fast and as hard as he could at the one player in the middle of the ring, the bull. The bull had to keep his feet chopping and turn quick to take on the hitters from wherever they came. Coach Renfro sent them at the bull pretty quick, so the bull also had to recover fast to get low enough to take on the next hitter.

Nathan was the most feared hitter as well as the most feared bull when he was in the ring. But when he was the bull, if you could get him before he turned to face you, or before he got his pads low, you could survive.

While they jogged in place, waiting for a turn to be called, Tate explained her plan.

"It's easy," she said. "You don't have to be there. You just gotta get your mom to help."

"Great," Troy said. "Just what she wants. She's already almost got fired because of me."

"You wanna hear the plan, or you wanna complain?" Tate asked over the cheers that erupted as Jamie Renfro ran out into the ring, knocking a smaller kid who was the bull onto his back. Jamie's dad switched the bull to the team's middle linebacker and called out Nathan.

Nathan growled and ran at the kid, knocking him so hard that he spun around before falling down. Nathan howled with his fists clenched and jogged back to his spot, grinning at Troy and Tate.

"Nice," Troy said, slapping Nathan high five, then turning to Tate. "Okay. Tell us the plan."

"You sit in the stands and watch," Tate said with a shrug, her feet pumping up and down in an easy rhythm. "You got a phone. She's got a phone. You tell her the play, she tells Seth. It all works."

"How's Seth supposed to hear her?" Nathan asked, removing his mouthpiece for a moment to speak more clearly.

"McGreer!" the coach screamed.

Troy didn't know if Tate realized it, but Coach Renfro always sent her out against Jamie and his two closest friends, while Nathan never got a shot at them. Jamie was out there now as the bull.

Tate sneered, lowered her shoulder, and out she went, crashing into Jamie Renfro only to be lifted up into the air and knocked back. She returned bouncing on her toes, though, happy just to have stayed on her feet.

"How does any middle linebacker get the plays they call?" Tate said, huffing and getting back into her place between Troy and Nathan as if nothing had happened.

"You mean the hand signals?" Troy said.

"Sure," Tate said. "Seth has to look at the sideline to get the plays anyway. Just have him teach your mom a few signals and she can let him know what play is coming."

"Too bad my mom won't even talk to him, let alone do some secret mission," Troy said.

"Why?" Tate asked.

Before Troy could answer, the coach yelled his name.

"Troy!"

Troy felt a fire spring up inside him. He ran at

Jamie full bore, ready to cream him. Instead of taking Troy on, though, Jamie dropped to the ground, cutting Troy's legs out from beneath him and sending him tumbling across the grass. Jamie and his friends laughed. Even Jamie's dad couldn't stop from chuckling and nudging one of his assistant coaches as he told Jamie in a loud voice that he was cheating.

That was all the father did, though. There was no yelling. No laps to run. Nothing.

Jamie was still laughing, looking at his friends, when Troy got up off the grass and barreled into him from behind, knocking Jamie down and leaving him in tears and gasping for breath on the fresh-cut grass. Jamie's dad went ballistic. He screamed at Troy for the cheap shot.

"What about what Jamie did to Troy?" Tate said.

The coach spun on her. His face was purple and a vein popped out in the middle of his forehead.

"You can run with him!" he screamed, pointing at the far goalpost. "Take ten!"

"Ten?" Nathan said.

"You go with them! And make it twenty! Or turn in your gear!"

Tate tugged Troy's arm and motioned her head to Nathan, and the three of them set out on a slow jog while all four coaches gathered around Jamie, helping him slowly up.

"Nice one," Nathan said, grumbling under his breath when they were out of earshot.

"He shoulda done it," Tate said, throwing an evil look at Nathan.

"I know," Nathan said, and hung his head. "But twenty friggin' laps."

"Sorry, guys," Troy said.

They rounded the goalpost before Tate swatted her leg and said, "So, you never told me. Why's your mom mad at Seth?"

Nathan was huffing loudly and didn't even lift his head.

"Money," Troy said, smashing a bloody mosquito on his arm. "She thought that he thought she was asking him for money. She blew a gasket."

Tate shook her head and kept running.

After their eighth lap, the rest of the team was turned loose. They got into their parents' waiting cars and drove off. The sun was long gone and the mosquitoes were having a feast. Jamie left with an assistant coach and his son. Mr. Renfro stayed put, though, with his arms crossed over his chest to watch them run the laps. Then Tate's mom got out of her car and marched over to him, probably to ask what was going on.

Tate wasn't paying attention to her mom. She seemed lost in thought, and suddenly she said, "So we get them together."

Troy watched Tate's mom as she began waving her arms in the air and yelling at Mr. Renfro, something about it being a school night and him being a maniac.

"My mom and Seth . . . get together?" he said absently, still watching Mrs. McGreer.

"Together," Tate said as they rounded the goalpost for the thirteenth time.

Tate's mom yelled for them to get into her car, that it was time to go home. Mr. Renfro shouted something at her, waving his arms over his head. When she snapped something back at him, he spun around and walked away. Troy, Tate, and Nathan stopped their jog and started to drag their feet toward the parking lot. Nathan groaned. Tate's mom had her hands on her hips, watching.

"Together, like a date?" Troy said, her words finally sinking in. "Are you crazy?"

"Don't worry," Tate said. "I know how this stuff works. Trust me."

She reached down into her sock and pulled out a folded-up piece of neon green paper. She unfolded it and waved it in their faces. It was the handout coach Renfro had passed out at the beginning of practice advertising the county punt, pass, and kick contest on Saturday afternoon.

"I was going to try this anyway," Tate said, "but now it can really help us."

"What the heck does *that* have to do with this?" Troy asked.

CHAPTER THIRTY

"LOOK AT FIRST PLACE," Tate said, holding it closer so Troy could see.

Troy couldn't kick or punt, so even though he could throw farther than any kid in his grade, he never bothered with the punt, pass, and kick contest. First place for the eleven-year-old group, besides a big golden trophy, was lunch with Falcons star linebacker Seth Halloway.

"It's for kids," Troy said.

"I know that," Tate said. "But if I can win it, I bet I can get your mom to go with me."

"How?" Troy asked. "What about your mom?"

"Look at the date for the lunch," Tate said.

"The Saturday after. So," Troy said.

"So, church," Tate said. "My parents go to adult

Bible study every Saturday from noon till two. You know my mom. She doesn't make exceptions. That's why half the time she misses our games."

Troy looked at Mrs. McGreer, standing there under the streetlight on the edge of the parking lot, hands still planted on her hips. She was short and stout, with Tate's olive skin and dark hair piled in a tight bun. An immovable force. Maybe the only person on the planet who could make Coach Renfro stop yelling.

"Maybe," Troy said. "But you gotta win."

"Win what?" Mrs. McGreer said, sliding open the door to her van so they could pile in.

"Just a contest," Tate said.

"Punt, pass, and kick," Troy said.

"I oughta punt, pass, and kick that Coach Renfro in the astronaut," Mrs. McGreer said, climbing in and starting the van. "Practice this late on a school night."

The three of them covered their mouths, stifling their giggles and nudging one another. Tate's mom never swore, but somehow she always got her point across.

The problem, as they saw it, was passing. Tate could punt and kick better than any boy her age, but her arm strength had never been a source of pride. They had just two days to get ready, but Troy thought he could help. The next day after school, Tate and Nathan got off the bus at Troy's stop. It was a warm and windy day with a clear blue sky. The pine trees waved and hissed over their heads as they walked down the twisty drive. Troy handed out cookies from the jar and poured glasses of milk for them around the kitchen table. Then they went outside to the bare spot and he lined Tate up facing Nathan, ten yards away.

"Okay," he said, handing her the ball. "Throw it."

She did. The ball wobbled its way toward Nathan, not even making it. Troy put his hand over his face but said, "We'll be okay. You just gotta get some spin on it."

"Spin?"

"A spiral," Troy said. "If you can throw a spiral, you can get it twice as far."

Nathan passed it back, delivering a wobbly knuckleball of his own that bounced off the dirt in front of them. Nathan smiled and shrugged. "I'm a lineman."

Troy showed Tate how to hold the ball with the tips of her fingers on the laces and then how to put a spin on it by rotating her fingers and wrist at the same time.

"It's in the wrist," Troy said, zipping a pass to Nathan, who dropped it and said, "Ouch."

Soon she got it, spinning the ball enough, not to create a tight spiral, but to get it wobbling in the right direction. Back and forth they threw it, dozens of times, until Tate said her arm hurt.

"Don't throw out her arm," Nathan said, "or we'll be doomed."

Troy nodded.

"Let's see how far you can get it," he said. "Then we're done."

They backed up to the pines and marked a line in the grit. Troy showed her how to get a bit of a running start and then heave the ball. Tate tried it and Nathan marked the spot in the dirt. Troy paced it off. Twelve yards. He frowned and brought back the ball, handing it to her.

"You gotta get mad, Tate," he said. "When you need to really chuck it, you gotta get mad."

"I'm not mad about anything," she said.

"Think of something," Troy said.

"What do you think of?" she asked.

Troy felt his face get warm. He didn't want to tell them he thought of his father, of being left alone. He didn't want to describe the vision of an imaginary figure walking out and slamming the door and tell them that's when he'd chuck the ball with all his might.

"Just think of something," he said.

"I know!" Nathan shouted, jumping up and down. He ran a few more yards away from them and turned his back.

"What are you doing?" Troy said.

"Give her the ball," Nathan said, looking back and doing something with his hands in front of him where they couldn't see.

Troy handed Tate the ball. Nathan dropped his

pants halfway down his butt and bent over, half-mooning them.

"You idiot," Tate said, scowling.

Nathan turned his head, grinning and sticking out his tongue, and spanked his backside.

Tate let out a roar and chucked the ball at him, crying out, "Jerk!"

"Pretty good," Troy said, pacing it off. "Fifteen yards. Not that bad, Tate."

"Happy to help," Nathan said, pulling up his pants.

"You *are* an idiot," Tate said.

"You won't say that," Nathan said, "when you win."

CHAPTER THIRTY-ONE

THEY WORKED THE SAME way on Friday, and Tate threw it fifteen yards again. Since she didn't turn twelve for another two weeks, Tate got to compete with a group of mostly fifth graders. On Saturday, after they played their football game with the Tigers, Tate, Nathan, and Troy took off their shoulder pads and trudged over to the field where the contest was being held.

The smells of grass and dirt mixed with grilling hot dogs and soda. Hundreds of parents and kids from all over Gwinett County milled about in the midday sunshine. In the middle of it all was a big white tent set up with tables underneath that were dressed up in red, white, and blue bunting. The trophies stood tall in gleaming rows, and Troy had a hard time taking his eyes off them. But when he looked over at Tate, he saw that her eyes were on the judges and a boy in a sleeve-less T-shirt heaving a pass as the crowd cheered.

Nathan pulled a piece of notebook paper out of his sock. It was sweaty from the game, but on it they could still see his smudged calculations.

"Last year, seventy-six total yards won it for eleven-year-olds," he said, pointing.

"Anyone we know?" Troy asked.

"Jamie Renfro," Nathan said, twisting up his mouth. "Remember? He brought the trophy into the lunchroom at school."

Nathan held the paper out for Tate and pointed to the numbers. "You can kick it farther than anyone—I say thirty-two yards. If you can get off a great punt, close to thirty, say twenty-eight, then you can win it with a decent throw. Heck, you did fifteen yesterday."

They all looked at the numbers and the grand total of seventy-six, which Nathan had circled. A thirty-yard punt would be amazing, even for Tate. The kick, she could do. She was doubtful about the pass, but she signed in at the table and started stretching her kicking leg.

Each kid got three tries in every event. The judges took the highest one. Nathan checked the standings at another table, and when he returned, his face was sagging.

"Sheesh," he said, shaking his head. "That guy in the cutoff sleeves got seventy-eight."

Troy looked at Tate, who acted almost like she didn't hear. The only way he knew she really did hear Nathan was that the tip of her tongue poked out between her lips. The only other time she did that was when she was taking a math test. It meant she was focused.

Tate's kicking was great. Her kickoff went thirty-three yards, the longest of anyone, and her punt was twenty-nine. She was one of only a handful of girls, and when the crowd saw her kick, they cheered loudly, sensing a winner. Tate beamed at Troy and Nathan as she walked from the kicking station toward the passing area. All she had to do was come up with a big pass and she'd have it. Seth Halloway was in her grasp.

"Get mad," Troy told her. He helped stretch her arm and then rubbed her shoulders, loosening them. "Sixteen yards, just one more yard than yesterday. Get really mad."

Tate scowled and hefted the ball. The judge held up his little red flag, and Tate nodded at him. Then, with a shriek, she ran at the line and heaved the ball with all her might.

Fourteen yards.

Nathan let out a groan. The crowd's applause was barely polite, deflated after her spectacular kicking. She came back with her head down.

"It's okay," Troy said, handing her a water bottle. "You're getting warmed up."

She nodded, but her lower lip disappeared between her teeth and her hair fell, covering the sides of her face. She clutched the shoulder of her throwing arm with her other hand. Troy lifted her chin and saw tears.

"What's the matter?"

She shook her head. "I'm fine."

She picked up the ball. Up went the flag. She gave a growl and ran at the line. Twelve yards.

"You gotta be kidding," Nathan said, and stamped away.

No clapping at all this time. The crowd sensed she was losing it.

Troy did his best to cheer her up, but it was no use. Tate's arm obviously hurt her, and worse still, he could see that her confidence was shot. But when she turned toward the line, Troy saw that Nathan had worked his way around the crowd and behind the open field, where the judge stood with his small red flag. Behind the judge was a hedgerow separating the grass field from the adjoining neighborhood.

Nathan had wedged himself into the bushes. He had his thumbs jammed into his ears and his fingers spread out and wiggling. He stuck his tongue out and crossed his eyes. Even under the circumstances, Troy had to laugh. He nudged Tate. She saw Nathan and shook her head.

"Very funny," she said, bending down to tighten her shoelace.

"Holy smokes," Troy said, the words spilling out of his mouth. He looked around in panic.

Nathan was going to get himself arrested.

He'd bent over into the hedge so that the only thing anyone could see was his naked butt, shaking the bushes.

Troy heard some of the ladies in the crowd gasp. A few of the men began to shout, and one of the officials started jogging toward the hedge. Troy winced.

"That *idiot*," Tate growled. The flag went up. She grabbed the ball from Troy's hands and chucked it with a war cry.

The judge nodded his head. This time the crowd cheered. Tate didn't know how good it was, but she knew it was close enough to make them measure.

Nathan had disappeared. The official peered into the bushes but came out empty-handed.

The judge had a helper who stretched out the measuring tape. The judge bent over the spot where Tate's pass had landed. He seemed uncertain and tugged at the tape again, making sure every bit of the slack was gone, then he checked it again and stood up to announce the distance.

Tate plugged her ears.

CHAPTER THIRTY-TWO

"**SIXTEEN YARDS, TWO FEET,** three inches," the judge said.

The crowd went wild.

Tate shook her hands in the air, but not to celebrate. She stomped back to Troy, scowling, and in a low hiss said, "I can't believe he *did* that."

"You won," Troy said.

"Yeah," she said, glaring at him, "the girl who threw to the moon. Everyone's gonna know. Thank God my parents aren't here. My dad will flip his lid."

Tate smiled at the judges, even though her face was red, and she accepted the big golden trophy along with the certificate to have lunch with Seth Halloway at Vickery's on Crescent Street in downtown Atlanta.

As the crowd began to leave, the two of them took their equipment as well as Nathan's and went to sit on the curb to wait for Troy's mom to pick them up on her way home from a special meeting she had at work.

"Where do you think he went?" Tate asked, looking around.

"He'll show up," Troy said.

And in fact, as Troy's mom pulled into the parking lot, Nathan stepped out of the bushes surrounding the park sign and slipped into the VW bug before either of them. Troy's mom asked about the game, and Tate told her they would have won if Coach Renfro had put Troy in. Troy's mom glanced over at him and patted his leg.

"Tate won the punt, pass, and kick," Troy said.

"You did? Congratulations," she said. "I know some of our players volunteered to have lunch with the winners. Who's your lunch with?"

His mom grinned at Tate in the rearview mirror. Nathan slouched down in his seat.

"Mrs. White," Tate said, "I need to ask you a favor. A big favor."

"What, honey?"

Tate told her how excited she was about her lunch but how her parents couldn't do it with her because of Bible study.

"Nothing comes between my parents and the Lord," she said.

"Certainly nothing wrong with that," Troy's mom said.

"And I got the player I love most," she said. "Not just because he's a great player, but because of all the nice things he does, you know, with sick kids and homeless people. Seth Halloway."

"Oh," Troy's mom said.

"He's my hero," Tate said, "and I was thinking, well, would you take me to the lunch? It says you have to have an adult."

Troy's mom glanced in the mirror. Her mouth was closed tight, and she blinked out at the road.

"I'll have to see about work," she said.

"It's like work, Mom," Troy said. "It's great PR, all the players doing this."

"I know it is," she said. "I actually put the sign up in the locker room and talked to some of the players about it. Maybe I can see if Seth could do it another time, when your parents are free."

It was silent for a moment before Troy quietly said, "Wouldn't it be easier just to do it instead of having to ask Seth a favor?"

His mom tucked her lower lip up under her teeth and put on her turn signal. They rounded a corner, and she nodded her head and said, "Okay, it's like work. I can do it."

They all cheered for her, and she smiled.

CHAPTER THIRTY-THREE

THE NEXT DAY, THE Falcons lost to the Saints in New Orleans. Troy watched the game with his gramp on the couch, leaning and groaning and covering his face with a pillow, knowing that he could have helped but that they wouldn't let him. That whole week, desperation grew inside him like the kudzu vines that swarmed the roadsides of Atlanta. Jamie's moronic "Falcons Suck" song and dance hardly bothered him. He had real problems to think about, because if the team didn't win, McFadden would be gone, and so would his mom.

The next weekend finally came, and at breakfast on Saturday, Troy asked his mom to drop him off with Nathan at the High Museum while she and Tate were at the lunch. His mom turned her head and looked at him from the corner of her eye.

"The museum?" she said.

"We're studying the Egyptians in school, and Mrs. Arnott said they've got real mummies at the museum. That's kind of cool, right?"

His mom nodded slowly and said of course she'd take them. The phone rang shortly after that. It was Tate, asking his mom if she minded meeting her there. Tate said that even though he couldn't miss the Bible study, her father wanted very much to meet Seth Halloway and that he would drop her off and then head right out to the church.

Troy felt a little guilty tricking his mom in so many ways, but they were doing it for her own good. If they didn't do something fast, she'd be out of a job before Halloween.

After she dropped them at the museum, Troy grabbed Nathan by the arm and started to run inside.

"What are you doing?" Nathan asked.

"We gotta see the mummies," Troy said. "So we can tell my mom we saw them."

They got directions from the guard and sprinted through the hallways until they came to the beginning of the Egyptian exhibit.

"They're kinda small," Nathan said, staring through the glass.

"Come on," Troy said, taking a look, then dragging Nathan by the arm.

Vickery's was a good six blocks away. By the time

they got there, his mom was already sitting on the brick terrace, alone with Seth Halloway.

Huffing and puffing, Troy and Nathan wormed their way in through the hedge on the side of the terrace and pushed up tight against the wall. The bricks were spaced in a way that left a two-inch gap between the next one, so Troy could not only hear what was going on, he could see.

Seth looked stiff, sitting there in a pale yellow polo shirt, his hair still wet, probably from a shower after the team's light Saturday-morning practice. Troy's mom didn't look much more encouraging. Her nose was buried in the menu.

She looked at her watch and said, "I'm sure she'll be here any minute."

"You'd think."

Seth looked around, and Troy knew they were talking about Tate. After a time, Nathan whispered into Troy's ear.

"Why aren't they doing anything?"

Troy pressed his fingers into the gaps between the bricks and held on. He closed his eyes and put his forehead against the cool, rough surface, willing his mom to look up at Seth and just smile. That's when her phone rang.

His mom answered it and said, "Tate? Where are you?"

Then she groaned and said she was sorry to hear that.

"Well," she said to Seth as she stood up, "she's not coming. Stomach bug. That's too bad—she was really excited."

Troy's mom extended her hand for a handshake.

Seth stood and shook her hand. Troy's mom gave it two quick pumps and picked up her purse, fishing for her keys.

Seth's face turned red.

"You know," he said, "we're here. You want to have lunch anyway?"

Troy put his knuckle into his mouth and bit down.

CHAPTER THIRTY-FOUR

TROY'S MOM LOOKED UP, trying not to smile. When she nodded her head, Troy held out his palm and Nathan slapped him five.

The boys listened to them talk, mostly about the Falcons. It wasn't until the check came that the topic changed.

Seth reached for the check and said, "Not to insult you, but I planned on buying lunch today anyway."

Troy's mom tilted her head. "I didn't mean to attack you like that," she said.

"I'm used to taking shots," he said. "That's how I make my living, remember?"

"Not from your friends, though," she said, her face turning color.

"So we're friends, huh?" Seth said, raising his eyebrows and wiping his mouth before setting his napkin on the table.

"Why not?" she said.

"Then we'll do this again?"

"Maybe," she said. "If you call me, I'll certainly check my schedule."

"Maybe? Wow. That hurts."

"I'm not one of these floozies who throws herself at you because you're a sports hero," she said. "Actually, I think that's somewhat of an oxymoron."

"I'm a moron now?" Seth said.

"No, an oxy-moron," she said with a chuckle. "Two things that are mutually exclusive—like how can someone involved in sports be a real hero? Get it?"

"Insulting," he said.

"I don't mean to be," she said. "I just think real heroes are soldiers and firemen and police, or teachers. Oh, I sound horrible. I'm sorry."

"No, that's all right," Seth said. "I think you're right."

"You do?"

"My dad was a cop," Seth said. "He got killed when I was three. There was a bank robbery."

"I'm so sorry," she said in a quiet voice.

Seth shrugged. "I never knew any different, really, not till later on. I guess that's why I know how Troy feels. You get to a certain age and it starts to hurt, not having that father there."

Troy felt his face get hot. He started to squirm and he wished Nathan wasn't listening. He tugged Nathan's arm and wiggled his way out of the bushes. The two of them stayed crouched until they reached the sidewalk.

"We better get back to the museum," Troy said.

"Yeah," Nathan said, nodding. "Good idea."

"It went good," Troy said after they'd traveled a block in silence.

"It seemed like they got along," Nathan said.

"At least enough so that she won't mind helping him, right?" Troy said.

They didn't stand in front of the museum for more than a few minutes before Troy's mom pulled up in her green bug.

"Where's Tate?" Troy asked.

"She got sick," his mom said.

"So how was it? Lunch?" Troy asked.

His mom didn't even look at him. She just said "Fine," and she had this dreamy look as she drove along, keeping her eyes on the road. Troy looked back at Nathan and winked.

At home Troy changed into his football uniform. The Tigers game didn't begin until five in the afternoon, and it was all the way out in Roswell. Troy didn't play, but it didn't bother him the way it usually did because he was thinking about the plan and how his mom was sure to go along with it, now that things were good with her and Seth. It didn't even bother him when Jamie ran a quarterback sneak into the end zone for an easy one-yard touchdown and then showed Troy the ball when he got to the bench as if he'd completed a fifty-yard pass.

It was late by the time he and his mom got home from the game. The sun had gone down behind a thick bank of clouds. His mom warmed up some lasagna and then made ice-cream sundaes with hot fudge and walnuts. Troy waited until the kitchen was cleaned up and they were just sitting at the table with a couple bottles of soda. It felt like the perfect time.

"He's a good guy, that Seth, huh?" Troy said, peering at her with one eye from around the edge of the pale green bottle.

"Yes. He seems to be," his mom said, setting her own bottle down and staring at him.

"What?" Troy asked.

"Just thinking," she said, turning the bottle around and around without moving it from its place on the checkered tablecloth.

"Me too," Troy said.

"Yeah?" she said. "About what?"

Troy tried to keep the excitement out of his voice. It was hard.

"Mom," he said, "you have to listen to this. I've got a plan."

CHAPTER THIRTY-FIVE

SHE LOOKED PUZZLED, BUT Troy couldn't worry about that. He plunged ahead, laying out his plan to use a cell phone to talk to her on the sideline so she could signal to Seth what the offense was about to do. He was speaking fast, desperate to get it all out so she'd see the beauty of it, so she couldn't say no.

"Troy?" she said, tilting her head. "Is that what it was really about?"

"What?" he said, doing his best to look dumb.

"You know what," she said, her voice getting softer. "You know."

"Not really," he said.

"Really, you do," she said.

Troy felt like he was on a hook and she was just reeling him in. He stared hard at the soda bottle, gripping it with both hands. Outside the window, the blue jay scolded something from its treetop.

"Do you know how *embarrassed* I am right now?" she asked him, her voice eerily calm.

"Why?" he asked.

She looked at him for a long time before she spoke. A crooked smile spread across her face.

"Because my son, my only son, is trying to trick me into doing something he knows could make me lose my job," she said. Her hands were out on the table now, clenched into fists and trembling. "Do you know I actually *hinted* that I'd go out with him again?"

"That would be good, right?" Troy said, his voice fading.

She pounded a fist on the table, rattling the cover of the sugar bowl and tipping over the salt.

"I am not a *toy*," she said.

"No one said that, Mom," Troy said, his eyes welling up with tears.

"You just won't let this stupid football thing go, will you?" she asked, roaring now. "Not until you've ruined everything. No, don't you cry. I'm the one crying here!"

Troy sprang up out of his chair and ran for his room, slamming the door and throwing himself on his bed. He strangled his pillow, then punched it, over and over, cursing under his breath. It was dark by the time his blood cooled.

He silently opened his door and walked softly out

into the living room. He could hear his mom's voice talking to someone out on the front porch. Through the window, he saw her sitting there next to Gramp's scarecrow, her legs curled up underneath her. She was talking on her cell phone. Troy crept close to the door, resting his face against the frame, listening through the screen. It didn't take long to figure out she was talking to Gramp, telling him what happened. Troy winced as he listened.

"Yes, he's very likable, Dad," she said, "but how much of it is real?"

Silence.

"I'm not underestimating myself, Dad," she said, lowering her voice to a whisper. "No one wants a woman with a twelve-year-old kid. They just don't. I faced that a long time ago."

Troy staggered back, a heavy knot twisting in his gut. His face went numb. His whole body went numb. His mom's voice was just a garble to him now, noise without words.

On his next step, he stumbled and bumped into the lamp. He grabbed for it, but too late to keep it from crashing to the floor. The screen door swung open and his mom stood there with a look of horror on her face.

"I gotta go, Dad," she said, snapping shut the phone. "Troy, I didn't mean that."

Troy just stared at her. The sound of the crickets outside was broken by the faraway groan of an oncoming train. They stood that way, just looking at each other.

Finally, she said, "I'm sorry I said that. I didn't mean for you to hear."

Nearer and nearer came the sound of the train, until Troy could hear the clack of the wheels.

"It's okay," Troy said, finding his voice. "I know what I am. That's why I want this so bad. I want to *do* something. I want to *be* something. I thought this was my chance."

The little jar of seashells his mom kept on the coffee table began to rattle and shake. Down in back of the house, the train rushed by in a vortex of speed and blaring sound, dying slowly away as it rounded the bend by the Hooch.

"I'm sorry I said no," his mom said. "You're right. Maybe this is your chance, and I want to help you take it."

CHAPTER THIRTY-SIX

THE CROWD IN THE Georgia Dome rumbled to life as the team took the field. Troy clenched Seth's cell phone in his hand and sat down between Nathan and Tate. Seth had gotten them tickets on the fifty-yard line. Troy searched the sideline for his mom and, as if she sensed him looking, she turned around and waved, pointing to her cell phone. Troy fumbled with Seth's phone and it slipped from his hands. Tate scooped it up and handed it to him, pinching it between her finger and thumb.

"It's all wet," she said, wrinkling her nose.

Troy wiped his sweaty palms on his pants and felt his face heat up. He dialed his mom and she picked up right away, looking at him as she did.

"All set?" she asked.

"I think so," Troy said. "You set with the signals?"

"Troy, between you and Seth I think I spent every free minute I had this week going over those things," she said. "I was doing them in my sleep last night."

Troy laughed at that.

"Call me when you know something, okay?" she said. "Good luck."

Troy felt like he was in a dream. The noise washed over him. The crowd cheered the Falcons and booed the visiting Oakland Raiders. He saw Seth come out onto the field and meet up with his mom on the sideline. She pointed at Troy. Seth gave him the thumbs-up. Troy raised his hand, then let it drop. Nathan leaned over him to buy a box of popcorn and a soda and had to shake Troy three times before Troy realized he was asking him if he wanted some. Troy said no thanks. The game began and Troy felt his insides go cold. The Raiders had the ball.

Troy gripped the edge of his seat, narrowed his eyes, and leaned forward. The Raiders ran the ball, then threw a pass. Two more runs. Two passes. Another run. Troy saw his mom look up at him from the sideline, and his stomach flipped. He felt his breakfast of scrambled eggs and ketchup boiling up into his throat and he choked it back.

Seth's words came back to him. If you can't do it under pressure, it's just a stunt.

"Relax," Tate said, offering him a bottle of soda. "You want a drink?"

"How 'bout popcorn?" Nathan said, stuffing a fistful into his mouth and spilling some onto the seats.

The Raiders completed a long pass on third down and got into field-goal range. The defense held them for three plays, then the Raiders lined up to try a field goal. The crowd sent up a wave of jeers. Troy pressed his hands against his ears, drowning out the noise, and concentrated. The Raiders' kicker missed and the cheers roared through Troy's hands. The Falcons' defense jogged to the sideline. Seth took off his helmet and looked up at Troy. Troy shifted his eyes.

A few seconds later, the cell phone rang. It was his mom.

"Are you okay?" she asked.

"Yeah," he said.

"Okay, honey, because Seth was asking me."

"I know," Troy said. "I'm trying. Something's wrong."

"Oh, honey," she said. "It's all right."

"Not really," he said. He felt those hot tears welling up behind his eyes. It made him furious.

"Was my father a crybaby too?" he asked.

"What?" his mom said.

"Nothing," he said. "I'll call you, Mom. When I see it."

He hung up the phone and bit into his lower lip. The Falcons drove down and tried for a fifty-two-yard field goal. They missed. The Raiders opened up with a long pass to Randy Moss. Touchdown. The Dome erupted in boos while Moss jiggled his backside.

The Falcons got the ball back, drove down, and made a short field goal. The Raiders took the kickoff and started to move, running five yards at a clip, completing almost every pass.

The crowd erupted and Troy looked down on the field. Randy Moss was in a shoving match with DeAngelo Hall. Yellow flags flew into the air. Both teams got penalized. The crowd's booing was like long, low thunder that just wouldn't stop rolling. Troy saw two wide receivers come off the sideline and head for the huddle as the fullback and tight end left the field.

"They'll motion Moss and throw a go route," Troy said, talking to Tate from the side of his mouth, his eyes intent on the field and the slouching, disrespectful body language of Randy Moss as he yelled and pointed his finger toward the referee. A "go route" was when the receiver used his speed and tried to just outrun everyone to the end zone.

"What did you say?" Tate said, grabbing him and shaking him.

"I said—"

"Call your mom!" Tate shouted.

Troy looked down at the phone and dialed. His mom answered, and he yelled the play into the mouthpiece. He squeezed the phone in his hand as he watched her. She was signaling to Seth, but he wasn't looking.

He must have given up.

But Troy's mom waved her hands furiously and got Seth's attention before dashing back behind the thick white line. Seth rolled his hands over in circles, motioning to Troy's mom to give him the signal again. She did, and Seth nodded and turned to the defensive huddle, pointing at Bryan Scott.

Moss sauntered back to the Raiders' huddle to hear the play, then they broke and came to the line. Moss went into motion. Troy stuffed a knuckle into his mouth. The quarterback snapped the ball and dropped into the pocket. Moss shot up the field. Troy saw Bryan Scott backpedal deep and drift toward Moss's side. The instant the quarterback started to throw, Bryan Scott took off toward Randy Moss. But the angle wasn't quite right. Moss was running too fast.

Even though Bryan Scott knew the play, Troy thought he wasn't going to make it.

CHAPTER THIRTY-SEVEN

TROY WAS RIGHT.

But it didn't matter. Even though Moss beat Bryan Scott to the end zone, the quarterback's throw didn't quite reach his receiver. Because Seth knew the play, he had blitzed through the offensive line and chased the quarterback, making him throw off balance. Bryan Scott spun, intercepted the wobbly pass, and ran it all the way back, ninety-one yards, for a touchdown. 10–7, Falcons.

"You did it! You did it! You did it!" Nathan and Tate screamed at him, jumping up and down and hugging him.

Tate kissed his cheek, and Troy felt tears spilling down the sides of his face, not tears of pain or fear, but tears of joy.

Pure joy.

Seth jogged to the sideline with his teammates, slapping high fives, head-butting, and hugging everyone around him. Troy kept his eyes glued to the old linebacker, so he saw Krock grab him by the front of the jersey and yank him close enough to say something into Seth's ear. Seth's face went dark. He shook his head, scowling at Krock, and walked through the cluster of players to the bench.

Seth looked up at Troy, gave him the thumbs-up, and winked with a big smile. Troy felt his insides glowing.

Troy's mom appeared and shook Seth's hand. He pulled her to him and gave her a quick hug. From up where he was in the stands, Troy saw Krock limping their way through the crowd of players. He sensed danger and knew Krock shouldn't see his mom talking to Seth. He dialed his mother, shaking his phone as if to make it ring faster.

She stepped away from Seth and answered.

"Get away from him, Mom," Troy said. "Krock's coming."

"Krock?" she said, taking another step back.

Krock broke through the wall of players and stood staring at Seth and Troy's mom. She turned her back to the coach, keeping the phone to her ear.

"What's he doing?" she asked Troy.

"Just looking at you," Troy said, hissing the words. "Walk away."

Slowly, she did. Krock eyed her for a moment, then turned his attention to Seth. Stabbing his finger at the linebacker, he began shouting.

"What's he shouting about?" Troy asked.

"He's telling him to play the defense that's called," his mom said, taking a quick glance over her shoulder. "He's saying Seth was supposed to cover, not blitz, the quarterback. I guess Seth changed the defense Krock told him to call after he got my signal."

"And he'll have to change it again," Troy said. "Rats."

"Seth can handle him."

"Let's hope. I'll call you when it's time for the defense to go out there, Mom."

Troy hung up and watched the Falcons' offense start to move the ball. They got to the fifty-yard line, and Mike Vick threw a perfect pass to Brian Finneran on a fifteen-yard crossing route. Finneran caught the ball but was instantly smeared by the strong safety. The ball popped loose and the Raiders recovered.

Nathan and Tate looked at him, and he nodded his head. The Raiders' offense came out and lined up in an I formation, running a simple run up the middle for a four-yard gain. Troy watched the field. The Raiders replaced the fullback with a third wide receiver. He dialed his mom.

"Draw play," Troy roared into the phone. "They're going to fake the pass and run right up the middle again."

Troy's mom had positioned herself right near the first-down marker, just as Seth asked her. She motioned her hands, signaling the play to Seth. The linebacker darted his head back and forth between Troy's mom and Coach Krock. He had to at least make it look like he was paying attention to the coach.

When Seth got the signal, Troy could see him shouting to his teammates. He was yelling and swirling his hand over his head like a cowboy in a rodeo. The Raiders lined up on the ball. The Falcons' defense started to crowd in. On the snap, everyone on the Falcons' defense blitzed through. Seth shot up the middle and nailed the running back just as he got the ball. The ball popped loose and a Falcons lineman came up with it, holding the ball high for the thundering crowd to see. The Dome shook under Troy's feet, and he and his friends hugged each other and screamed at the top of their lungs.

Mike Vick threw a touchdown pass to Alge Crumpler on the very next play. The place went wild.

After the kickoff, the Raiders went back out on offense, down now 17–7. Troy watched the people they sent out onto the field and dialed his mom, telling her they'd run a sweep play to the right. His mom signaled Seth, and the defense tackled the Raiders runner for no gain.

"Yes, Mom! Yes!" Troy shouted into the phone, pumping a fist into the air.

But Troy's mom didn't hear. She was jumping up and down with the cell phone in her hand, cheering along with everyone else. Troy was smiling down at her when Krock appeared, shoved her, and snatched the phone out of her hand.

The coach put the phone to his ear, and his voice snarled at Troy over the line.

"I know you're up there, boy," the coach said, gazing up toward the stands, "but you're finished!"

CHAPTER THIRTY-EIGHT

KROCK HELD UP HIS mom's phone and snapped it in
two. Troy watched him hand the broken pieces back
to his mom and then limp away. His mom looked
down at the broken phone for a moment with her
mouth open, then she faded back into the crowd of
photographers as if to hide. To Troy, it was almost
like a silent movie.

He turned his attention back to Krock, who was
signaling Seth over to the sideline. The crowd cheered
the old linebacker as he jogged off. Krock's face was
twisted and red with rage. Krock pointed to the
bench, motioned for Seth's backup to get out onto the
field, and turned his back on Seth. Seth didn't budge.
He started yelling and waving his hands at the coach
until Krock spun around and jabbed his finger into

Seth's chest, screaming something and pointing to the bench again.

When Krock turned back toward the field, Troy saw Seth march right over to Bart McFadden and grab him by the upper arm, obviously telling him what had happened. McFadden frowned and nodded and walked with Seth over to where Krock stood watching his defense. The Raiders snapped the ball and threw a pass to the tight end for a fifteen-yard gain.

Krock spun around when he felt Bart McFadden's hand on his shoulder. Krock smiled wide. The two coaches began to talk when, suddenly, the crowd erupted. The Raiders had just scored a touchdown, making it 17–14.

Krock went crazy, pointing at Seth and pointing to the bench before he stormed away. McFadden said something to Seth before he walked away too.

Seth turned and threw his helmet down. It bounced off the turf and rolled under the bench. Seth followed it and sat down, his chin resting on the breastplate of his shoulder pads. They had benched him.

Troy turned his attention to his mom and saw her ease through the photographers and up behind the bench, showing the security guard her pass as she went. She put her hand on the backrest of the bench and knelt down behind Seth so none of the coaches or other players could see her. She said something to Seth, and he slowly turned around and shook his head. She gestured at him with her hands, pointing up toward Troy, then back to the field. Seth looked at her, smiled, and started nodding.

The crowd suddenly erupted in deafening boos. Troy looked to the field. The Raiders had intercepted a pass and run it in for a touchdown. The Raiders now led, 21–17.

When Troy looked back, his mom was talking with one of the security guards, who took a cell phone out of his pocket and handed it to her. She looked up at Troy, and the phone rang.

CHAPTER THIRTY-NINE

"**WHAT DID SHE SAY?**" Tate asked when Troy ended the call.

The stadium was a blur of red and black and a funnel of noise. Troy tried to focus, but he kept expecting that he would wake up and be in his bedroom. It was all too weird. Tate shook him.

"They want me to go to Mr. Langan," he said, still staring.

"The *owner*?" Nathan said.

Troy nodded. Tate looked up at the luxury boxes, scanning for a moment before she pointed and said, "There he is."

Troy turned his head. Sitting there next to his wife was John Langan, severe looking in his dark suit and red tie, gazing down at the field, his neat, thin mustache a flat line above his tightly closed mouth.

"But how do you get up there?" Nathan asked.

"Come on," Tate said, dragging Troy out of his seat. "If she says we have to go, then we have to go."

Troy followed her up the concrete steps and into the concession area. Tate walked a little ways and yanked open a teal-colored door opposite the hot-dog stand. Concrete steps and a metal railing went up as well as down.

"This is the emergency exit," Nathan said.

"So it has to go to all the floors," Tate said. "Come on."

Their footsteps pinged off the concrete, echoing through the stairwell. They went past the door on five all the way to six. Tate tugged on the handle.

It was locked.

She turned to them and said, "Okay, when they open this door, we have to think fast and talk fast. We can't take no for an answer. Troy, remember, your mom works for the team. She told you to find Mr. Langan, and he's going to want to see you. You just keep telling them you *have to* see him, and Nathan and I will help."

"How?" Troy asked.

Tate smiled and shrugged. "We'll figure a way."

Then she began pounding on the metal door and shrieking at the top of her lungs. Still, it was nearly five minutes before the handle turned and the door jerked open. A woman security guard in a dark blue vest with a silver badge peeked her head through the door.

"What in the world?" she said.

Tate slipped through the opening and darted behind the guard, causing her to turn. Troy and Nathan followed them out into the carpeted hallway. A curving line of doorways went for as far as Troy could see in either direction. Opposite the doors was a metal railing that opened out over the club lounge a level below. There were other guards, sitting in chairs facing the doors every fifty feet, and the two closest stood up and started their way holding walkie-talkies.

"You children can't come on this floor unless you're sitting in a box," the guard said. She grabbed Tate's collar. "Now come on."

Tate shrugged her off and stamped her foot, pointing at Troy.

"His mom works for the team," she said, her face pinched and red. "We're supposed to be here."

"I'm supposed to see Mr. Langan," Troy said, straightening his back but unable to keep his eyes from shifting toward the approaching guards and his voice from sounding weak.

"If your mom works for the team," the guard said, squinting at them, "where is she? Where are your passes? Uh-uh. You three go right back down where you came from."

That's when Nathan grabbed his own throat and fell to the floor. He began choking and groaning and twisting his whole body like he was doing the Worm

Dance. His eyes rolled up into his head. The one guard stepped back, her face aghast. The other two ran up and knelt beside Nathan, trying to hold him and squawking into their radios at the same time.

Tate screamed at the top of her lungs and shouted that her friend was dying.

CHAPTER FORTY

TATE GRIPPED TROY'S ARM and yanked him away from the little crowd.

"Go!" she yelled into his ear, pointing at the curve of doors. "It's gotta be one of those. Go!"

Tate shoved him away, then turned, stuffed her fingers in her ears, and started to scream again.

Troy felt like he'd had an electric shock. He was scared to death. Still, he put his hand on the first door he could reach and pulled it open. A man in a tweed blazer with a glass of wine in his hand looked surprised.

"Is this Mr. Langan's box?" Troy asked.

The man looked him up and down and scowled, but he shook his head and pointed with his thumb, saying, "Two down. What's going on out there?"

Troy yanked the door shut and darted away. Tate's screaming pierced his ears. Another guard dashed past Troy, nearly knocking him over. Troy glanced back and saw a pair of emergency medical technicians bursting out of the elevator next to the stairwell in their white coats. Troy walked fast, two doors down, and tried the door. It was locked.

Troy looked around the corner of the little alcove, back out into the hallway. It was chaos. Tate was still screaming, but two of the guards had her now and she was kicking her feet wildly in the air. A policeman got off the elevator this time. The EMTs were bent over Nathan, trying to hold him still.

Troy dipped back into the alcove and knocked on the door. When no one answered, he knocked louder. When that didn't work, he pounded with his fists. That's when a tall, angular man in a suit appeared. Troy had seen him with Mr. Langan before—Bob McDonough, a former Secret Service Agent. His eyes were blue and hard, and he turned them down on Troy and asked him what he was doing.

"I have to see Mr. Langan," Troy said, swallowing.

Bob McDonough heard the noise and leaned out into the hallway.

Troy made a move to slip past, but Bob McDonough seemed ready. His hand clamped down on Troy's shoulder.

"Where are you going?" Bob McDonough asked.

"I have to see him," Troy said, pleading. "My mom works for him. He'll want to see me. Something's happening down on the field. He's going to want to know. Please."

Bob McDonough narrowed his eyes and said, "You're that kid. They dragged you out of the Cowboys game."

Troy shook his head. "You have to tell him. Tell him Troy White. My mom is Tessa. Please. He'll want to listen. I know he will. Please."

Bob McDonough looked out into the hall again, then frowned at Troy.

"Wait here," he said.

The door closed. The lock clicked.

Troy put his hands against the smooth wood and rested his face against its cool surface, pressing his ear tight but hearing only the roaring noise of the crowd as something exciting happened out on the field. He felt the door handle vibrating, someone unlocking it. His heart jumped and he stepped back, smoothing his shirt.

But before the door opened, a woman's voice behind him shouted, "That's him! That's the kid!"

He spun and stared into the angry face of the security guard.

Beside her was a police officer with handcuffs.

CHAPTER FORTY-ONE

"WHAT'S GOING ON?" BOB McDonough asked.

The police officer took Troy by the shoulder and put one hand behind his back, snapping open one of the handcuff bracelets.

"These kids were trying to get to Mr. Langan," the cop said.

"We got them," the security guard bellowed. "I stopped them all."

"Wait," Bob McDonough told them.

Troy stood frozen. The security guard folded her arms and scowled at him. Bob McDonough took the cop by the arm and led him around the corner, into the hall. The two of them whispered back and forth, the cop eyeing Troy until he nodded and put the handcuffs back on his belt.

"Come on," Bob McDonough said to Troy, walking past him and back into the luxury box.

They walked through a sitting area with a table of food and a bar against the back wall. Two waiters hovered uncertainly. There were three tiers of seats going down on either side of a small set of stairs. Troy saw men in suits and, in the front row, Mr. Langan with his own young son and his dark-haired wife. The owner's eyes were glued to the field.

The scoreboard said the Falcons were now even further behind, 24–17. Mike Vick dropped back. Every receiver was covered and the defensive linemen were breaking through. Vick darted one way, then the other, dodging defenders and weaving through his own players toward the line of scrimmage. Mr. Langan jumped to his feet along with the other seventy thousand people inside the Dome. The noise was so loud that Troy could feel it in his teeth.

Then a Raiders linebacker clipped Vick's ankles and down he went for no gain. The air went out of the crowd. Troy swallowed and moved toward the owner.

"Wait," Bob McDonough said, clamping his hand on Troy's shoulder.

They stood, watching the Falcons' offense sputter until they finally had to punt. What energy was left disappeared and the Dome seemed to deflate while everyone waited for the TV time-out to end.

"Okay," Bob McDonough said, moving Troy toward Mr. Langan.

There was an empty seat, and the owner told Troy to sit down. He introduced his wife, Allison, and his son, Sam. Troy was confused. It was as if Troy had been invited, but the comfort of the owner's politeness melted after Troy had shaken hands with Sam.

Mr. Langan turned to him with a serious face and said, "I like your mom, Troy, but why are you here?"

Troy's throat got tight, and his first few words seemed to squeak out of his mouth. He told the owner about Seth, how the linebacker had asked for Troy's help, that he didn't know why but he knew things were going to happen in a football game before they did. He told him about meeting Coach McFadden and how Coach Krock threatened to make him look bad. And he told him why Seth Halloway was no longer in the game.

As Troy finished his story, the Falcons kicked off and the owner cast his eyes down onto the field. As the kickoff team came off, the defense ran on and Seth stayed on the bench.

"I know it sounds crazy," Troy said, "but it's true. Look. Why would he take Seth out? He was playing awesome."

Mr. Langan looked at him for a minute, and Troy was certain he was going to be kicked out. But instead, the owner reached out to the low wall in front of him and lifted the receiver of a red telephone off its hook. He glanced at Troy once more before leaning forward and staring down at the field.

"Get me Coach McFadden, please," Mr. Langan said into the phone.

Troy leaned forward too and watched the commotion in the bench area. The ball boy who had answered the red phone on the Gatorade table scrambled for the head coach. McFadden pulled off his headset and took several long, quick strides to reach the phone.

"Bart," the owner said into the phone, "is Seth Halloway hurt?"

There was a pause before he said, "Then why isn't he in there?"

The owner nodded and said, "Then get him for me."

Mr. Langan kept his eyes on the bench area and the phone tight to his ear. Troy watched as the head coach marched over to the sideline where Krock was directing the defense, giving hand signals to the backup middle linebacker. When Coach McFadden got there, Krock shouted at him and waved him away. Bart McFadden walked back to the Gatorade table alone.

As the owner listened, his brow wrinkled until he was scowling darkly. He thanked Bart McFadden and hung up. Then he looked at Troy before standing and heading up the stairs. When he reached the top, he turned back to Troy and said, "Are you coming?"

Troy jumped out of his seat and dashed up the steps.

CHAPTER FORTY-TWO

NO ONE ASKED TO see their passes now. Bob McDonough moved through the Dome, a dozen paces in front of them, clearing the way. As they passed the security checkpoints, Troy felt the guards' eyes boring into him and he wondered what had happened to Tate and Nathan. He wanted to ask Mr. Langan, but the dark look on the owner's face left Troy's tongue in a knot.

Right out onto the field they went, marching up the thick white sideline. Troy had to hustle to keep up. Krock was angled away from them, signaling to the Falcons' defense, which now had its back to the far goal line. But instead of going to Krock, Mr. Langan went straight over to the bench. Seth Halloway stood up and tossed half a cupful of Gatorade into the big trash can.

"Is it true?" Mr. Langan asked.

Seth looked from Troy to the owner and nodded.

"Krock *wants* us to lose," Seth said. "Troy knew what they were going to do. That's how I made those plays.

"I know it's bizarre," Seth said, shaking his head, "but it's true. He's, like, some kind of football genius."

At that moment, the crowd began to boo. Randy Moss was in the end zone again. Mr. Langan's mouth twisted up.

"Come on," he said to Seth.

The two of them marched over to Krock, picking up Bart McFadden on the way. Troy followed.

"Coach?" Mr. Langan said, folding his arms across his chest. "I want Seth back in the game."

Krock's eyes widened and their brows shot up.

"I'm sorry, Mr. Langan," he said. "I know you're the owner, but I'm the defensive coordinator. Halloway's not running the defenses I'm calling, and like we say back home, that dog don't hunt. You can't run a football team like that. I can't."

"You don't have to," Mr. Langan said. "You're fired."

Krock's mouth dropped. He looked at Seth, then the owner, before stabbing his finger at Troy.

"This kid? This kid is trouble," he growled, white flecks of spittle spraying from his mouth. "You're crazy. All of you! You don't fire Carl Krock because some snot-nosed kid thinks he's a mind reader."

Mr. Langan glanced back at Troy and said, "This has nothing to do with Troy. I make the decisions with this team. You're done."

Krock clenched his fists and took a step toward Troy.

"Don't you even think about it."

"Mom," Troy said. His mother stepped between him and the coach, her chin up high.

"I'll tear your eyes out," she said.

Krock stopped and shuddered, his face turning bright red. Finally, he tore his headset off and smashed it to the ground. He pushed past them, then stopped and pointed back at Troy.

"You're done too," Krock growled at him. "Don't think you're not."

Krock stormed out of the bench area. A reporter came up to him with a microphone. Krock grabbed the man by his shirt and shoved him back into his cameraman, knocking him to the turf. The crowd of reporters and cameramen stepped back and made a lane for Krock as he limped toward the locker room tunnel, snarling and showing them all his fist.

Troy turned back to Mr. Langan, Seth, and Coach McFadden with an expectant smile, but they were talking in a tight group and not paying attention. Troy nudged the carpet with his toe, waiting for them. His mom put her hand on his neck and gave him a squeeze.

On the field, the Falcons' offense had sputtered and they were letting the clock run out to halftime. Just as both teams streamed off the field toward their locker rooms, Seth peeled off from the little group on the sideline and walked toward Troy.

Troy looked past him at Mr. Langan. The owner's eyelids were closed halfway, and he put his hand to his chin, considering Troy.

Seth made a pounding motion in the air with his fist and, grinning, said to Troy, "They're gonna try it."

CHAPTER FORTY-THREE

MR. LANGAN WALKED OVER and said, "Don't worry, you'll get your chance after halftime."

Troy's mom cleared her throat and said she was supposed to get the first-half statistics from the press box for the coaches.

"Go ahead," the owner said. "Troy, you want to go into the locker room and listen?"

"Sure."

His mom hurried off.

"Oh my gosh," Troy said when he was alone with the owner. He felt like he'd been hit by a bolt of lightning. "My friends."

"Friends?" Mr. Langan said.

Troy explained what happened to Tate and Nathan, how they helped him get past the security guards.

"The police took them?"

Troy nodded.

"Oh. I think I know where they'll be," Mr. Langan said with a frown, signaling to Bob McDonough. "Come on."

Troy followed the team's owner and his security director down the sideline and into the tunnel. They followed the concrete tunnel a quarter of the way around the Dome until they came to a door where a policeman stood guard.

"Any customers?" Mr. Langan asked the officer.

"Just a drunk who took off his clothes and tried to get out on the field, and a couple kids who tried to break into the luxury suites," the officer said.

"Good," Mr. Langan said. "I think they're the ones we're looking for."

The officer opened the door for them. Inside the large concrete room was a desk where a policewoman sat reading a book. Across the back wall were several mini jail cells. In one, a drunken man in boxer shorts lay sprawled out on his back. He was singing the national anthem so loudly that his big gut shook like a mountain of Jell-O.

In the next cell, Tate sat in the corner with her hands over her ears. Nathan had a tin cup in his hand and was rattling it against the bars, shouting at the drunk to be quiet.

Troy figured the policewoman was reading a pretty

good book, because Mr. Langan had to shout at her several times above the noise before she looked up, then jumped to her feet in surprise.

"What?" she asked.

"I said, I want you to let these children go!" Mr. Langan shouted.

"I can't do that," the officer said, shaking her head. "I'm sorry, but I got orders."

Troy saw Mr. Langan's face turn red, like he was about to explode, when a police captain walked in with Bob McDonough. The captain shook Mr. Langan's hand and apologized. He told the officer to set Tate and Nathan free.

"Sheesh," Nathan said, running his hand through the bristles of his crew cut and rolling his eyes. "Get me outta this crazy place."

The drunk continued his bawling and the officer went back to her book. On their way out into the tunnel, two more officers arrived, dragging an older man between them. The man's face was painted red and black, and he talked in an endless stream of words with his finger pointed in the air, telling them how they had to let him see Mike Vick before he was abducted by aliens.

"See what I mean?" Nathan said as they headed down the tunnel, following the owner.

"I thought they'd take you to the hospital," Troy said.

"He blew his cover," Tate said, glancing bashfully up at Mr. Langan, "and his lunch. All that popcorn too."

"You woulda blown your cover too," Nathan said. "Sheesh, and your lunch. They were gonna do a tracheotomy. That thing where they cut a hole in your neck so you can breathe? When I saw that knife, I blew my lunch and my story, but I'm sorry, I wasn't lettin' no ambulance jockey cut a hole in my neck."

Tate gave Nathan a look of disgust, rolled her eyes, and said to Troy, "It was a pocketknife. They tricked him. Man, did it smell. All over the paramedic."

Mr. Langan was smiling, but he cleared his throat and asked them if they wanted to stand with Troy on the sideline.

"Sure," Nathan said, "but can I get a dog down there?"

He pulled some wadded bills out of his pocket and said, "I got money."

"I thought you were sick," Tate said.

"Naw," Nathan said. "I gotta reload. A hot dog and a soda and I'll be fine."

Mr. Langan laughed and asked Bob McDonough if he could find something to reload Nathan, then he looked at his watch and said they better get out on the field, as halftime was almost over.

CHAPTER FORTY-FOUR

THE THREE OF THEM followed the owner out onto the field, and only Tate didn't seem slightly embarrassed with the way everyone, even the players, moved out of their way. Mr. Langan said that it would be best if Tate and Nathan stayed back behind the bench with Bob McDonough. Nathan slapped Troy a high five and Tate pecked his cheek.

Troy blushed and turned away to look up at the scoreboard. The Raiders were leading 31–17, and they were going to receive the kickoff.

Seth appeared, swishing water in his mouth before leaning over and spitting it into a garbage can. Troy's mom arrived too, and folded her arms across her chest. Out on the field, the Falcons' kickoff team crouched down with their hands on their knees, ready to go.

"We set?" Seth asked.

The whistle sounded and the action began.

"If it's okay with you," the owner said to Troy, "you and I can stand with your mom and she can give the signals you've worked out to Seth and we can see if this really works."

"It works," Seth said, his voice urgent. "He knows."

"Well," the owner said, putting his hand on Seth's shoulder pad, "we'll see. Go ahead and get in there and let's win this game."

Seth bent down so he was face-to-face with Troy.

"We're on, buddy," Seth said, gripping Troy's shoulders. "Let's show them."

Seth snapped up his helmet and jogged out onto the field.

With Mr. Langan next to them, the players cleared a path and Troy and his mom got right up to the edge of the field. He stared out at the Raiders' offensive formation and explained to the owner that he needed to get into the rhythm of the game.

"The Raiders probably made some changes at halftime," Troy said. "Everyone usually does."

After each play, he looked up at Mr. Langan's expectant face, winced, and shook his head. He was aware that his mom was there beside him too, her face lined with anxiety. Troy wanted so badly to show the owner what he could do that his head began to pound.

The Raiders' offense was on the move, and after each play, Seth would look over at them, but everything was different from the first half. Troy felt the knot in his stomach tighten, and he thought he was going to have to run back to the garbage can to get sick. He took a deep breath and let it out. The Raiders ran eight plays straight and ended up kicking a field goal.

Seth jogged off the field with the rest of the defense, patted Troy on the back, and said, "You'll get it. Relax."

Seth looked the owner in the eye and said, "Halftime adjustments. He'll get it."

Mr. Langan put his hand to his chin and nodded his head without saying anything.

CHAPTER FORTY-FIVE

THE FALCONS' OFFENSE TOOK the field.

Inside the bench area, right in the middle of it all, Troy could feel the energy. Coaches yelling for players to go on or come off. Players arguing, or celebrating with hugs and cheers and shoulder slaps, sweat dripping from their faces and limbs, spattering each other when they spoke. Blood ran from noses and deep cuts that went unnoticed by them, and up close Troy could see the crimson stains that speckled their jerseys and pants.

It was like stepping into the battle scene of an action movie. The Falcons' offense moved a little but ultimately stalled and punted. Seth and the defense took the field, and Troy's focus shifted back to the Raiders' offense.

On the second play of the series, there was a scream at the end of the play. Everyone froze. One of the Falcons' linebackers was lying on the turf right near the sideline, rocking slowly like a leaf on the roadside before it gets lifted away. The crowd went quiet, and Troy could hear the player howling in pain.

The doctors and trainers ran out and surrounded the injured player. The ref blew the whistle, signaling a TV time-out. Troy edged closer, fascinated and horrified at the same time. The linebacker's elbow bulged in a funny way and the forearm jutted sideways at a crooked angle. The trainer knelt and held the player's shoulder. The grim-faced doctor took his lower arm in both hands and gave it a quick, firm tug. Troy heard the joint pop back into place. The player grunted and his eyes rolled back for a second before he got up and staggered to the bench.

A whistle blew and the game resumed. The next few plays only confused Troy even more, and he felt the tight grip of fear in his stomach turn to panic. Was his gift like a loose lightbulb that sometimes would work but sometimes wouldn't? Seth kept looking anxiously over at Troy, but Mr. Langan kept his eyes on the field now and seemed to have given up.

Troy looked back at his friends. Tate and Nathan grinned at him and nodded their heads like broken puppets.

He nearly smiled, and he felt the knot loosen just a bit.

Two plays later, the light came on.

He felt a jolt, and the joy of seeing it, feeling it, of knowing what was going to happen, warmed him from the inside out. The strategic adjustments the Raiders had made in the locker room at halftime were suddenly clear.

He looked at his two friends. He grinned at them and pointed at his own head, nodding as hard as they had, then he looked up at the owner and touched his arm.

"Think you got something?" Mr. Langan asked.

"Oh, yeah," Troy said. "I got it all."

"Great! Let's see it," the owner said, and he signaled Troy's mom to do her thing.

Troy told her it was a slant pass to the wide receiver on the weak side of the formation. She nodded and signaled in to Seth. She held up her left hand with four fingers splayed wide, their signal for the weak-side wide receiver, and made a diagonal slashing motion with her right hand for the slant. Seth quickly changed the defense, shouting and slapping the backside of one of his big linemen to get into the right position.

The Raiders snapped the ball. The Falcons' strong safety blitzed the quarterback, who rushed his pass, and Seth hit the receiver running the slant with a blast that lifted him off his feet and sent the ball bouncing off the turf. The crowd exploded, and Mr. Langan slapped high fives with Troy and his mom.

It was so loud and Troy was so excited that Mr. Langan had to take him by the shoulders and turn him back to the field to watch for the next play. The yard marker said it was third down with five yards to go for a first. He saw another receiver run into the huddle and the tight end run off. He smiled and chuckled because it came to him so quickly and easily.

"Draw play," he said to his mom. "Strong side."

The Raiders broke their huddle and jogged to the line. His mom made a motion like she was scribbling with a pen to signal the "draw" play, then made a muscle with her right arm to signal strong side. Seth bounced on his toes as he shouted the change in the defense, and Troy was bouncing right along with him, literally jumping off the turf.

When the ball was snapped, Seth made a beeline for the strong side. Troy turned his shoulders and leaned, the same as Seth did as he slipped through a gap in the line. Then Troy dropped his hips and threw his arms around the air in front of him, just as Seth did the same to the runner, lifting him off his feet and driving him back to the turf. The crowd went wild. Intoxicated by the deafening thunder of applause, Troy leaped forward and ran halfway out onto the field as Seth came running off with a swarm of teammates around him. Seth wrapped his arms around Troy and lifted him in a bear hug, bounding off the field and mussing his hair and roaring all at the same time.

"You did it, buddy! You did it!" Seth screamed, setting Troy down beside his mom and ignoring the jostling smacks his teammates put on his shoulder pads and back.

The offense caught the excitement and the crowd kept it up too, despite the gaping lead that the Raiders had. The momentum was back with the Falcons. Mike Vick scrambled and threw rocket passes. Warrick Dunn darted, shook, and blasted his way down the field until they were in the end zone.

Seth was amazing. Even though he knew the plays with Troy calling them and his mom signaling them in, the excitement of what they were doing seemed to make him run faster and hit even harder. The Raiders could do nothing on offense. Every play they tried, inside runs, outside runs, short passes, or long passes, Seth and the Falcons' defense were ready and waiting. After stopping the Raiders' offense, Seth would run off the field with his fists raised and the crowd cheering him, and he would go right to Troy and slap high fives until Troy's hand hurt and his cheeks were sore from grinning.

The Falcons' offense, inspired by the devastating hits of their dominating defense, kept up their part of the bargain. They moved the ball up and down the field, almost at will. By the time the gun sounded, Atlanta had the win they so desperately needed, 40–34.

Seth's final stats totaled seventeen tackles, two interceptions, and two quarterback sacks. When his teammates carried him off the field on their shoulders, he pointed at Troy, giving him a thumbs-up, and grinned like a crazy ghoul with the black rubber mouthpiece covering his top teeth.

Troy's mom hugged him. Her laughter bubbled up around him, swirling with the cheers of the crowd and the hearty war cries of the enormous players. Nathan and Tate pounded him on the back. He was dizzy. It was louder than the lunchroom and happier than Christmas morning. It was a light-headed excitement unlike anything Troy had ever felt before.

CHAPTER FORTY-SIX

TROY'S MOM MADE HIM put on a shirt and tie when they went to see Mr. Langan in his office the next day before school. Troy stared out the bug's window at the Falcons' facility, tugged at the itchy collar, and yawned. His mom had let him stay up late to watch the halftime show of the *Sunday Night Football* game. She, Seth, and Troy all sat there together on their couch, giddy at seeing Seth's spectacular replays as the highlight of the show. When the announcers raved about how the Falcons had overcome their first-half flop with a nearly flawless performance after halftime, Seth had crowed, "That's my man!" and made Troy blush.

As they pulled up to the guard shack at the Falcons' facility, Troy asked, "What do you think he's going to say?"

His mom just waved to the guard and shook her head.

The owner was wearing a suit. He stood up behind his desk and offered them a drink, and then the two chairs facing his desk, before he sat back down.

"What you did yesterday was great," he said to Troy, "and I'd love it if you could go through the rest of the season with us. The only problem is people finding out about you, for a lot of reasons, not the least of which would be other teams finding out. Carl Krock *was* a problem, but I think I've got that worked out. If he ever wants to coach again after what he did to that reporter yesterday, he's going to need a recommendation from me and he knows it.

"But what about you, and what about your friends?"

"They won't tell," Troy said. "My mom told them the same thing yesterday—that we shouldn't talk about it. And why would I?"

His mom nodded.

Mr. Langan pondered a moment, then said, "What would you think if I hired you for the rest of the season as a ball boy? That way you could be on the sideline without attracting attention."

Troy's heart seemed to swell, and his head swam.

"That would be great," he said.

"I can't see paying you fifty dollars a game, though," Mr. Langan said, staring hard at him. "I was thinking ten thousand."

Troy blinked.

"A game," the owner said.

His mom gasped and put her hand to her chest.

"Mr. Langan," she said.

He held up his hand. "I imagine Troy will want to go to college one day."

"On a scholarship," Troy said.

"Well, you'll figure out something."

CHAPTER FORTY-SEVEN

TROY DID HIS THING, and the Falcons won their next two games. The team was ecstatic; so were the fans. People were starting to talk playoffs now, and Troy's mom opened a bank account for him that had twenty thousand dollars in it. More, she said, than she'd ever seen in one place at one time. Troy thought the thrill would last forever, but it didn't, and he tried to put his finger on just why not.

He thought maybe it was because he wanted so badly to tell Jamie Renfro that it was him and Seth Halloway together who were turning the season around for the Falcons. But he was pretty happy just because their winning had put an end to Jamie's stupid song and dance about how bad the team was. He thought maybe it was because he had to keep the fact that he was a football genius a secret. But the people who mattered most knew. Tate. Nathan. His mom. Gramp. And Seth.

Then it hit him. Even though being a part of his favorite NFL team was a dream come true, there was another dream that hadn't. It was his own team, the Duluth Tigers. He was still sitting on the bench Saturday afternoons, watching while Jamie played quarterback. Troy didn't tell anyone, though. He figured one dream was more than most people ever got. Still, it bothered him.

One thing that didn't bother him was his mom and Seth going out to dinner or the movies a couple times a week. It was fun to see his mom getting ready, then see Seth blush as he came through the door. Then, one evening after dinner, Seth showed up at the house unannounced.

Troy was already dressed for football practice and throwing balls at the tire when the big H2 rumbled up the drive and shuddered to a halt. Seth got out slowly and limped across the dirt.

"What's it feel like?" Troy asked.

"What?" Seth said.

"Your body," Troy said, nodding toward his knees. "After a game."

Seth stopped and looked down at his legs. "Like someone took a hammer and hit every bone, joint, and muscle in your body. That's about it."

"I guess the money makes it worth it," Troy said.

"The money's good," Seth said. "I'm not going to pretend. But that's not why you play. You don't do this to yourself for the money."

Seth pointed at the golf ball–size welt on his forearm.

"It's a dream," Seth said. "It was my dream, anyway. And, not to sound like an old man, but in this world it seems like you don't get to have too many dreams come true. So you ice down and you take your medicine and you keep living it."

Troy nodded. He was quiet for a minute, then he said, "Hey, Seth, what about when you first got the dream? Did it seem like, after a while, you wanted more?"

Seth gave him a funny smile and said, "Some people are driven. That's just how they're wired. They drive for one thing, then they get it and they need to drive for something new. Yeah, I know exactly what you mean."

The screen door swung open and his mom came out. She was wiping her hands on a dish towel.

"Mean what?" she asked.

"Just talking about dreams," Seth said. "Speaking of which, can I talk to you for a minute?"

"I was just going to take Troy to football practice," she said. "I was thinking about sticking around and watching a little, to see how bad this Jamie Renfro really is."

"He sucks," Troy said.

"Troy," his mom said.

"Well," Troy said, shrugging, "he does."

"Let's talk nice," she said.

"Okay," Troy said, sounding prim and proper. "He's *awfully* bad."

"I guess that's better," she said.

"Well?" Seth said.

Troy noticed for the first time that in Seth's hand was some kind of envelope. Troy's mom glanced at it and asked Seth if he wanted something to drink.

"Coke, if you got one," he said.

Troy let them go, then quietly opened the screen door and slipped inside. Something was up. Quietly, he peeked into the kitchen.

His mom popped the tops off two bottles and set them on the table. Seth took a seat, and she sat down across from him.

He took a sip, then stared at the Coke bottle for a minute, smiling stupidly.

"I . . . well," Seth said, putting the envelope on the table and pushing it across to her, "I don't really know how to ask you, but next is our bye week. We've got four days off, and I was thinking about getting away. Bermuda's supposed to be this great place. There's a beach with pink sand and this lighthouse where you have tea, and the water's as blue as a blue crayon, and . . ."

Troy's mom stared down at the envelope. Seth pushed it farther toward her before returning his hands and his eyes to the pale green Coke bottle, which he slowly rotated in its place.

His mom opened the envelope and removed a stack of papers. She examined the one on top.

"First class to Bermuda," she said, her voice quavering. "Seth, I can't."

She stuffed the papers back into the envelope and pushed it back across the table.

"It's not that I wouldn't like to," she said quietly. "I'm flattered, but I can't. I'm a mother, and I can't really be more than that right now. Troy needs me. And you know what? Honestly? I need him."

CHAPTER FORTY-EIGHT

TROY WANTED TO SHOUT, but he bit into his cheek and clenched his hands.

Seth's face turned dark red. He took a deep breath and let it out through his nose as he nodded his head. He got up from the table without looking at her.

"Thanks for the Coke," he said.

"The tickets," she said, picking up the envelope and holding it out toward him.

Seth stopped and looked at it.

"It's all paid for," he said. "I can't get my money back, and the truth is, if I can't go with you, well, I've got work to do around the house anyway.

"We can still work together, right?" Seth said. "I mean, Troy and the whole football genius thing? I don't want you to feel uncomfortable."

"Of course we can," his mom said quietly.

Seth nodded, gave her a quick smile, and headed for the door. Troy darted through the living room, down the little hallway, and around the corner. When he heard the screen door bang shut, he went into the kitchen through the other way.

His mom sat staring at the envelope on the table. She took a deep breath and let it out slow.

In a soft voice, Troy said, "What happened, Mom?"

"Nothing, honey," she said lightly, but without looking at him.

"You should go, Mom," he said. "I don't want to be the reason you aren't happy. I can stay with Gramp, you know."

She stared at him for a moment, then said, "Honey, if I don't have you, I don't have anything. You're my life, Troy. I'd die for you."

She stood up, took the envelope, and slapped it against her leg. It burst open, spilling its contents onto the kitchen floor.

"Darn it," she said, kneeling down to clean up the mess.

One of the tickets had slipped halfway under the stove. Troy knelt down in his football gear and reached for it. When he pulled it out, the cover caught the metal lip underneath the stove, tearing the cover free from the ticket.

Troy looked down at the ticket and his heart

jumped. He blinked and shook his head and blinked again. He held the ticket up closer to his face: TROY WHITE.

"Mom," Troy said, holding it out to her. "This is for me. He means me, too."

"You?" she said, taking it and examining the name.

She rifled through the mess of papers in her own hand.

"Me," she said. "Seth. You. A room for us and a room for him . . . Seth."

Outside, the H2's engine roared to life.

"Seth!" she shouted, jumping to her feet and racing for the door.

Troy jogged after her, amazed at how fast she was. The H2 was turning the bend. Troy's mom leaped from the porch and took off in a sprint, chasing the dusty cloud down the winding drive, yelling his name at the top of her lungs until the H2's taillights glowed and the truck pulled to a stop.

His mom waved her hand in front of her face, coughing and sputtering as she rapped her knuckles on the driver's-side window. Troy caught up to her and saw Seth's long face as he rolled down the window.

"Yeah?" he said.

"You mean all three of us?" his mom said, her voice pitched high with excitement. "Troy too? To Bermuda? All of us?"

Seth's face broke out in a giant smile.

"Of course," he said, glancing at Troy and nodding like an idiot. "That's what I said."

"No," she said, "you didn't. You didn't say all three of us."

"I didn't?" he said. "Well, I got three tickets."

"I know," she said, jumping up onto the running board. "I know that."

His mom leaned into the window. She wrapped her arms around Seth Halloway's neck, laughing, and kissed him on the lips.

CHAPTER FORTY-NINE

TROY WAS RIDING HIGH up in the passenger seat of Seth's H2 as it pulled into the parking lot and rumbled to a stop facing the practice field. He looked back at his mom and smiled, but was disappointed when he saw that the team was already gathered around the coaches at the far side of the field. He had hoped Jamie would see them arrive and him hopping out of Seth's big truck.

He sighed and pressed his lips together in a frown, then kissed his mom before he hopped down, thanked Seth for the ride, and waved good-bye without looking back. He ran across the field to his team and kneeled between Tate and Nathan.

"Troy, it's real nice of you to join us," Coach Renfro said, sneering at his watch. "Especially since you're the new Falcons ball boy and the team rules don't apply to you anymore.

"Now that everyone is here," Coach Renfro added, "I have an announcement to make."

Coach Renfro's face scrunched up and got dark. He took the whistle off his neck and began to spin it around on his finger. His voice got louder and louder with each word he spoke.

"It seems some parents aren't very happy with my coaching style," he said, glaring at Troy, Nathan, and Tate. "It seems some people think it's more important that I baby some people than win games. We're out of the playoffs, and that doesn't matter to some people.

"Some people are more concerned with me *yelling* at their little babies!" he shouted, throwing his whistle down and stamping on it. Then he got quiet. "Some people went to the league president and complained, and they finally came up with their little pansy verdict. So I'm not coaching this week's game."

He directed his gaze at the three dads who were his assistants and said, "And if I'm not coaching, I assume my staff isn't going to be coaching either."

The other fathers' faces were grim, and they nodded their heads.

"So," Jamie's father said, "no coaches, no game. We're just going to have to forfeit, and since it's the last game, we'll say good-bye to the season right now. I'm sorry."

The entire team turned their heads to glare at Troy and his friends. Tate was toying with her chinstrap and wouldn't look up. Nathan's face was pink, and he studied his hand. Troy felt sick, but he glared right back at them, absorbing the brunt of their hatred, until he heard someone behind him clear his throat and say, "What time's the game on Saturday?"

The deep man's voice startled Troy as much as anyone. Coach Renfro's eyes popped out of his head and his mouth fell open; so did all the kids'.

One of the other coaches said, "The game's at eleven."

"I've got to catch a plane to New York, but it's not till three. I'll coach it."

Troy spun around.

Standing there with his thick arms folded across his chest and a tough-looking grin on his face was Seth Halloway.

CHAPTER FIFTY

BACK BY THE TRUCK, Troy could see his mom, shading her eyes from the sun, watching.

"Real nice," Coach Renfro said in disgust, "but we already made our decision. Come on, Jamie."

Jamie got up and followed his dad to the parking lot. The three assistant coaches looked at one another.

"You guys will have to help me a little," Seth said. He knelt down and dug Coach Renfro's whistle out of the grass, then dusted it off and made a little chirp. "But I kinda know what I'm doing and I know we got a good line—"

Seth winked at Nathan.

"—the best kicker in the league—"

He winked at Tate.

"—and one heck of a quarterback."

Seth angled his head toward Troy. The fathers grinned at Seth and, one after another, stepped forward to shake his hand.

"So," Seth said, giving the whistle a blast. "Let's line up and run some plays."

The Tigers jumped up, and Seth walked out onto the field to set a ball down on a line. He told the first-string offense to line up and asked one of the dads to put a defense across from them.

"The thing you want to do when you're sizing up an offense," Seth said, speaking in a voice that rang out across the grassy field, "is know how deep you can go with your passing game. Who's the fastest receiver we got?"

Rusty Howell raised his hand.

"So let's throw one deep," Seth said. "Rusty, you just go as fast and as far as you can. Troy, you let it fly. Now, I want the defense to put a rush on, 'cause I don't want Troy to be able to stand back there all day. Okay, on two, let me see it."

Troy shook the feeling into his arms and put his mouthpiece in. He slapped his own leg to make sure it was all real, then he stepped up to the center, glancing out at Rusty Howell, who gave him a thumbs-up and a grin. On the sideline behind Rusty, Troy's mom waved.

"Down!" Troy roared, beginning the snap count. "Set! Hut! Hut!"

The ball snapped up into his hands and he dropped back seven steps. Rusty took off in a blur. Ten yards.

The defense began to close in, pushing Troy's linemen back toward him.

Twenty.

Rusty looked back and held one hand up high. Troy had the ball up by his ear, cradled in both his hands like a pro.

Thirty.

He'd never thrown it farther than thirty-eight yards, and that was when he was raving mad.

Forty.

He cocked his arm. There was no rage fueling him now. It was something else, a blinding energy he never knew he had.

Forty-five.

He snapped his hips, rotating his entire body, funneling that energy up through his arm and out through the very tips of his fingers, rocketing the ball into the air.

The whole team turned their heads to watch. They saw it spin. They heard the laces whistling and the slap of the ball when it smacked down into Rusty's outstretched hands, and Troy heard them gasp.

Troy stood limp, empty now, as if it weren't really him who'd thrown such a pass.

The only thing left was his smile.

I AM GRATEFUL TO THE NFL for the use of the Atlanta Falcons name. Because I played for the team, this means a lot to me. However, FOOTBALL GENIUS is a work of fiction and the events and characters in this book, other than those football players mentioned who are public figures, have come from my imagination.

I would like to thank my agent, friend, and adviser, Esther Newberg, for bringing me the idea to write this book. Also, I couldn't have done it without the fabulous editing and enthusiasm provided by Barbara Lalicki and her team, especially Laura Arnold. Nor could I have done this without the valuable input from my son, Troy, and my daughter, Tate, and her teacher, Mary Arnott, who allowed me to test market the book by reading it aloud to her class as I wrote. Young readers Colin Fitzsimmons, Sam Morkal-Williams, and Jake Feerick also provided helpful input.

I would also like to thank art director David Caplan and designer Joel Tippie for the touchdown they scored with the design of this book and its cover, as well as my old friend and photographer, Jimmy Cribb.

A special thanks to my good friend Arthur Blank,

and his wife, Stephanie, who generously allowed me to use his team, the real Falcons, as the backdrop for this story and for welcoming me into the Falcons family as if I were a current player.

TIM GREEN, for many years a star defensive end with the Atlanta Falcons, is a man of many talents. He's the author of such gripping books for adults as the *New York Times*–bestselling THE DARK SIDE OF THE GAME and a dozen suspense novels, including EXACT REVENGE and KINGDOM COME. Tim graduated covaledictorian from Syracuse University and was a first-round NFL draft pick. He later earned his law degree with honors. Tim has worked as an NFL analyst for FOX Sports and as an NFL commentator for National Public Radio, among other broadcast experience. He lives with his wife, Illyssa, and their five children in upstate New York. FOOTBALL GENIUS is his first novel for young readers.